HIS PLEDGE TO OBEY

A SILVER STAR RANCH ROMANCE

SHANAE JOHNSON

CHAPTER ONE

"Wow, soldier, you sure do put the fox in foxhole."

Jackson Bennett's brow furrowed in a wince. He was sure the woman aimed for a sexy purr with her voice. What came out was more of a wet cat's screech. Along with the assault on his ears, Jackson's nose wrinkled in distaste at the rancid smell of alcohol wafting from her parted lips. He wouldn't have been surprised if that foul tongue of hers couldn't hold up against the rag the bartender was using to wipe down the greasy bar.

"Do you even know what a foxhole is?" he found himself asking before he could think better of it.

The Screecher grinned. Or at least Jackson

thought that was a grin. To him, it looked like a crooked slash across the bottom of her face.

Instead of waiting for her answer, which Jackson knew would be both wrong and inappropriate, he answered his own question. "It's a hole in the ground where soldiers seek shelter from enemy fire."

"Hmmm." Her next purr attempt sounded like a yowl. "I'd like to crawl into a hole with you."

"Yeah, well, this fox is spoken for." Jackson gave her his back as he took the drinks offered up by the bartender.

When he turned to head back to his table, there was still an irate feline blocking his way. He should've known better. Cats moved when they wanted, not when they were dismissed.

"I don't see a ring," she said, eyes peering at the two mugs in his hand.

Jackson held the two tumblers away from the Screecher in case she tried the age-old tomcat retaliation of knocking a drink over with her claws. In doing so, the bare skin below the knuckle of his left hand was clearly on display, showing its ringless state.

Nobody had put a ring on it yet. Because his

fiancée hadn't said she liked him yet. But they were getting married. It was just that he and the woman he had promised to marry hadn't met face to face yet.

"Oh, you're just engaged."

The Screecher came dangerously close to Jackson's drinks. He pulled them back to his chest defensively. His eyes narrowed on her long, painted nails.

"Want a fling before you tie that knot?"

Jackson had had enough. He'd had enough of women giving him unwanted attention. This was the fourth one tonight. He'd thought he'd affected a stay-back kind of attitude, but he guessed the women in town took that as a challenge.

Jackson turned and slammed his drinks down on the bar. The impact of the thick glasses coming down on the hardwood reverberated up and down his arms. The sensation wasn't painful. However, it was enough to wake up the other aches and pains in his body. There were many.

"Did you just feel the earth move?" said the Screecher. "I imagine you'll be just like a surprise earthquake when I get you back to my place."

Somehow her hands were headed straight for his belt buckle. In the middle of a crowded bar, no less.

Jackson was done with this outing. He'd had his arm twisted into this sociable excursion, and now he was being attacked by this wildcat. This was why he was a dog person.

With a flick of his wrist, Jackson disarmed the hellion and ducked out of harm's way. Once out of the foxhole of the bar, he stepped right into enemy fire.

Bodies marched left, right, then swiveled around in an about-face to repeat the moves again. The formation and synchronized steps reminded him of his time in the military. Though there wasn't that much shimmying and shaking in Boot Camp.

Jackson didn't know the moves of the line dancing that had most of the patrons up and on their feet. Even if he did, he wouldn't have joined in. The mere thought of moving so quickly made his knee ache.

He hadn't moved that fast in over a year. He might not ever be able to move that fast again. Not with the injuries he'd sustained during his time in the Armed Forces.

Jackson didn't begrudge a single ache or pain. He'd saved countless innocent lives and served with honors. Had a Silver Star medal to prove it.

What did bother him was that his injuries prevented him from going back and serving the greater good. The shrapnel that had lodged into his right knee on his last mission had left a lasting impression, one of constant aches and pain.

He wasn't quite thirty years old, yet he was already washed up. Ready to be set out to pasture like many of the horses on the Silver Star Ranch. There was more in him, more he could do for his country. But his body just wasn't up for the task. Not on the battlefield and not on the dance floor.

Jackson skirted around the quick-stepping bodies and made his way over to the table of his friends. Though he could hardly see his buddies. Wilson had his arms wrapped around his new wife, Mareen. Their dark heads were together as they alternately spoke into each other's ears and stole lingering kisses.

Beside them, his former team leader Linc and his wife, Scout, shared one chair. The newlyweds also spoke to each other as though no one else in the world existed. Their words were also interrupted by lingering kisses to the mouth.

This was why Jackson had gone to the bar. He was surrounded day in and out by happy couples trying to sneak off for privacy, which was near impossible when nearly a dozen people lived on the Silver Star Ranch. Sure, the ranch was sprawling with enough space. But the living quarters were simply too close for comfort now that there were three sets of newlyweds to contend with.

Jackson would be one of those newlyweds. Hopefully, soon. But he doubted he and Gunnery Silver would share the same chair, much less the same country. The sigh that escaped his mouth didn't sound like hope. It was a sigh of resignation.

This was the decision he'd made. It was all that was open to him now. He couldn't go back into the military. Not with his bum knee. He couldn't stand sitting at a desk and working the intel channels. Though he could no longer jump out of a plane, or swim for miles, or trek through a jungle, Jackson Bennett was still a man of action.

Much slower action, maybe. Action on even ground, probably. And no sudden movements, definitely.

The only action left to him was to marry a woman he'd never met. A woman he'd never even spoken to. All so that he could have a place on the Silver Star Ranch where he at least felt of use. The arranged marriages had worked out well for three of his buddies. Odds were it would work out for him too.

"What about this guy?" Carter Shane brushed his overly styled hair away from his brows.

It was a move Jackson had seen Korean pop stars effect that would make teenyboppers lose their minds. The woman sitting beside Carter, in her own chair, didn't notice. Artillery Silver's head was focused on the phone she held between them.

"Are you kidding?" said Tilly. "He's wearing a Hawaiian shirt. I wouldn't be caught dead with an 80s reject."

"Not everything in the eighties was bad," said Carter.

Tilly's blonde head shot up as she looked at him in shock.

Carter held his look of nonchalance for one second longer. Then he grinned and chuckled.

Tilly shoved him in the shoulder. "I almost believed you."

"Get real," Carter scoffed. "As if I'd let you marry a fashion-don't."

Carter bumped Tilly's shoulder as his gaze returned to the phone. Tilly bumped his back as her attention returned to her phone's display. Jackson caught the tilt of Carter's head and the flare of his nostrils as he leaned just an inch too close to the woman.

"Where's Brig?" asked Jackson. When Carter didn't raise his head, Jackson repeated the question, his voice an octave higher.

"Who?" said Carter, gaze still on Tilly's phone.

"Your fiancée," ground out Jackson.

Carter looked up then, but he didn't move away from Tilly. "Oh, right. She's..."

Jackson spotted her before Carter found her. Brigadear Silver was on the dance floor. She stepped in time to the beat, following the formation of the line dancing. She swiveled her hips and flipped her hair in a move that made Jackson swallow hard.

The impact of his gulp landed with such a resounding thud in his gut that he felt it in his kneecap. That was nothing to the jolt that registered when Brig caught Jackson's gaze. That mischievous grin that was always near her lips spread wide. She raised a hand and crooked a finger at him.

Jackson felt his body move unbidden. His legs straightened, a near-impossible feat with his injury. His toes spread in his boots. His heels flexed as though he was already marching toward the dance floor, toward her.

Something in his mind told him to stop, to halt, to about-face. That way lay a minefield. But like always, he couldn't help himself when it came to the youngest Silver Sister. Something about Brig drew him near.

Luckily, when Jackson looked down, he saw that his body hadn't moved from the chair. He still sat in it alone. Which was how he was going to stay.

Brig was off-limits to him. Not just because he would be marrying her sister in a matter of weeks. Because he had nearly ten years on her.

That became even more evident when Jackson saw a young man move in front of Brig. She placed her hand on his shoulder and swayed with him. It had been the young man she'd been calling. The man without a touch of premature gray in his hair. The man without a knee problem that kept him from being able to dance those quick steps. The man who wasn't washed out of the only career he'd known just before his thirtieth birthday. Jackson turned away from her.

Brig wasn't meant for Jackson. She was meant for Carter. Carter, who was closer to her age. Carter, who didn't have a physical injury, though he still had issues of his own. Carter, who should be doing something about that young buck who was dancing with his fiancée while moving his hands into enemy territory at Brig's low back.

But Carter wasn't paying attention, so Jackson would have to step in.

CHAPTER TWO

"Thanks for the dance, Barry."

Brigadear Silver shoved the roving hands off her bottom as she watched Jackson turn away from her. What did she have to do to get the man's attention? She was in her best dress. This dress had gotten her out of a speeding ticket, a C on her last history exam, and drinks at the bar from the bartender who knew she was underage.

But apparently it had no effect on the one man she wanted to notice her. Anytime Jackson saw her coming, he turned the other way. Whenever she spoke, he always looked down. She didn't think he disliked her. She caught the grin each time she told a joke or made a witty comment that made others pause and repeat in their heads what she said before they got the joke.

Those witticisms often made others stare at her quizzically. Not Jackson. His brow always lifted when she said the unexpected. So much so that she expected he was the only person who actually understood her.

As the baby of the Silver sisters, no one listened closely to Brig. Most times, her sisters gave her a pat on her head when she offered any advice. Only to turn around moments or days later, relaying what she'd initially suggested to them as though it was their own idea. It had stopped bothering Brig, who never cared about the credit.

Until Jackson showed up.

Brig didn't want him to look at her as though she were a child. She didn't want him to think she didn't have the brilliant mind that put her first in her Occupational Therapy classes. She was the youngest person in the Master's level courses, having finished her four-year Bachelor's in three years.

She was used to hitting the books hard. She always found the answers either in the text or at the back of the book. She wasn't having such luck trying to crack Jackson Bennett's code.

Her fiancé was worthless in getting any information out of. All Carter cared about was what he put in his hair, or the clothes on his body, or making fun of guys on dating apps with Tilly. Which was likely what he was doing now.

Tilly and Carter had their heads together. The two had grown as thick as thieves as they ran a commentary on the men Tilly measured for marriage in her app.

Carter wasn't a bad guy. He was actually pretty cool. That is, when he paid attention to Brig instead of her sister. Brig had never fought for Carter's attention, not like she was fighting for Jackson's.

How could she not fight for Jackson's attention? He had the kind of eyes that bored into a girl. His muscles were more like a bear's than a man's. And that touch of gray at his temples made Brig shiver even when she wasn't on the dance floor. There was something about gray-haired men that did it for her.

Brig had a type. And that type was older men. She knew she had issues. She'd studied psychology as a minor, after all.

"Ah, come on, Brig, let me buy you a drink."

Brig's attention fell back to the young man in front of her. She'd forgotten Barry was even there. "I'm too young to drink."

She'd be twenty-one in just a matter of months,

but she'd already tried plenty of alcoholic beverages. She didn't like most. Beer tasted like potatoes to her. Wine tasted like rubbing alcohol. She'd never understood the draw.

When she was just a girl, her sisters had ordered her a Shirley Temple. That fruity, fizzy concoction had remained her drink of choice to this date. She had no qualms about ordering it in a bar. She just preferred a tall drink of something else right now.

"One more dance," said Barry.

His hand was on her hip. Low on her hip. Brig did not like the grip. It was far too possessive for her. This was another reason Brig didn't like to date boys her age. They were still learning manners.

"Come on," Barry said. "You know you want to."

Those were five of Brig's least favorite words; *you know you want to.* Being the youngest of six sisters, everyone thought they knew better than her. Most of the time, Brig went along because she was often the one who planted the idea to begin with.

Take tonight, for example. She'd casually mentioned how hard they'd all been working all week to Scout when they were re-shoeing a horse, which was Scout's least favorite job on the ranch. Then she'd brought up how none of the now married men had had a bachelor party, and wasn't that a shame, while the guys were mucking out stalls. Finally, she'd hung up the flyer of the town's most popular -and only- bar on the fridge before dinner last night.

And here they all were. Except, the actual plan had been to get Jackson to dance with her. Unfortunately, he hadn't ventured anywhere near the dance floor all night long.

Brig had been throwing down a lot of her best moves on the hardwood. The DJ had started the night playing Hannah Montana's *Best of Both Worlds* and just finished up with Miley Cyrus's *Party in the USA.*

Now playing was *Blurred Lines,* the song Miley made famous with a certain dance move on a music awards show. But Brig was not in the mood to twerk. And certainly not with Barry.

"Good night, Barry."

Brig made to shove past the man. Boy, really. Barry couldn't have weighed much more than her. In fact, she probably had a few pounds on him. She had half an inch on him, and she was wearing boots, not six-inch heels.

Instead of letting her pass, Barry grabbed her arm. Brig whirled, preparing to throw a punch. She was too late.

Barry was already backing up with his hands raised. Fear in his wide gaze. An apology spewing from his lips.

Brig turned, expecting to see a big, brown bear of a man coming to her rescue. Instead of tall, dark, and handsome, she was met with four women with blue eyes blazing.

"I know you did not just try to force yourself on my baby sister," growled Scout.

Brig wanted to argue that she wasn't a baby. But she knew they wouldn't hear her. Even though the music had come to an abrupt halt.

"Sorry, sorry." Barry backed up at the same time as he looked for backup.

The crowd of men looked away or shook their heads sadly. This was one of the reasons that Brig and her sisters had had trouble finding husbands, even boyfriends, before the President's Men had come along. Her family had a bit of a reputation. No one messed with the Silver sisters without taking their lives into their own hands. And that included dating one of them.

Carter stood with Tilly's phone in his hand. His body angled toward hers as though ready to throw himself into harm's way to protect her and not his fiancée. That didn't bother Brig one iota. Something else caught her attention.

Jackson hung on the sidelines, watching it all go down. She saw that his hands were clenched into fists. Linc had a hand on his shoulder as though holding him back. So, tonight hadn't been a complete bust after all. Jackson did feel something for her, as evidenced by his stance and fists.

The seed she'd painstakingly planted had taken root. Now Brig just had to fan that seedling by throwing fire on it to make it grow. Water was for the faint of heart.

It was a start. This, coupled with what she had planned for Monday morning, should get her closer to her goal.

CHAPTER THREE

It felt like a tank was sitting on his legs. The pressure weighed Jackson down, making him want to stay in bed long after the sun rose. At the first light of day, he hefted himself out of bed.

His knees made popping sounds as he bent them to throw his legs over the side of the mattress. He let his right leg hang off the side for a moment. The joint creaked and groaned as it swung like a door, unsure whether it wanted to be open or shut. If only a bit of oil would quiet this ball and socket.

Jackson reached for the medication on the side table. With a shake, two pills popped out of the bottle and into his palm. Two was the recommended dose. Jackson put one pill back in the container and popped the remaining one in his mouth.

The aches and pains were manageable today. The thought of becoming addicted to the pain meds was not. He'd seen far too many hardened soldiers bend the knee to that cruel mistress.

Unlike insurgents, Fentanyl didn't sneak up on soldiers. No, she walked right into camp. She was handed out to soldiers to manage their pain. Little did they know they were welcoming friendly fire.

Opioid addiction wasn't a new thing in the armed forces. As far back as the Civil War, soldiers had self-medicated. The advent of morphine had brought relief from more than just physical injuries. With the pain and stress a soldier took on, that mental escape offered by morphine and later synthetic opioids was welcome. Jackson was far more fearful of succumbing to that trap than he was of losing his knee.

He capped the meds and shoved them out of sight. The relief to his joints was near-instant, but it wasn't absolute. The pain cleared enough for him to get on with his day and think clearly.

Most soldiers stayed away from hard drugs. They'd lose their livelihood in the Armed Forces if it was found out they were using. But worse, using could also get them killed when all their faculties weren't online in the theater of battle.

Jackson was no longer in the fog of war. He was on another battlefield. He was trying to pave a path for the rest of his life. One that he could walk without tripping himself up. He was pretty sure that he was headed in the right direction now that he'd arrived at the Silver Star Ranch. Though walking out of the bedroom of the cabin he was staying in and into the living room, Jackson had a moment of doubt.

Posters lined the walls. They proclaimed everything from Save the Whales to Meat is Murder and Don't Support Circus Cruelty. It was as though the animal rights organization PETA had been the interior decorator for the place. Or this had to at least have been a haven for their organizational meetings, complete with yoga mats, meditation rugs, and bean bags.

This hadn't been Jackson's first choice in cabins. When he and Truman had opened the door a few weeks ago, the former sniper had backed up and run to the last cabin on the row. That left Jackson stuck here in Gunnery Silver's cabin.

He was set to marry Gunny next month. He'd already set up house in the cabin she'd built with her father and sisters. But he'd never had a conversation with the woman.

Jackson introduced himself to Gunny over email a couple of weeks ago when the Silver sisters and the President's Men had hatched this arranged marriage plan so that they could keep the ranch. If all six sisters weren't hitched by the General's deadline, then the ranch would pass to his ex-wife, an unpleasant woman who couldn't wait to turn them out and turn the ranch into something like a parking lot. Gunny's response to Jackson's thoughtfully worded email, "Fine. I'll be there in a few weeks. But after the vows, I'm out."

Well, that did wonders for his ego. But what did he expect? To find true love like Linc and Scout? Or Jeff and Saylor? Or Wilson and Mareen?

He knew love wasn't in the cards for him. Not when he couldn't sweep a woman off her feet if he wanted to. He could barely maintain his own weight.

This was the best he was going to get. He'd give his vow to Gunny. Keep his pledge. And soldier on along this new path.

Decision reaffirmed, he paced the length of the cabin a few times. At first, his right knee wouldn't stand any weight he put on it. His knee always took a few minutes to warm up in the morning. Like a car in winter needing to idle before raring to go.

He felt no pain thanks to the medication. Just because he couldn't feel the pain didn't mean his body worked perfectly. With each determined step, Jackson's knee relaxed a bit more. His movements became smoother and less stiff. Once he stepped outside, he was walking normally.

"It looks like he has arthritis in the knee."

Jackson paused, nearly stumbling as he came to a halt. Brig leaned against a railing. Her gaze was on him, as it often was when they were near each other. She looked lovely in a sundress and flats. He rarely saw her out of jeans and boots. The outfit made her look professional, older, like a woman he might consider bringing closer to him.

"He's not showing any of the signs, Brig," said Scout.

Scout's attention wasn't on Jackson. She and Saylor were eying one of the horses. Colonel Brandon was the horse's name. Jackson knew that because the horse was a trained dancer. He hadn't known that such a thing was possible until he saw Mareen leading the horse in high stepping, choreographed movements.

"I don't see any swelling in the carpus or the

tarsus," said Saylor, her gaze traveling from the horse's front and then back legs. "I don't hear any popping or grinding as he walks."

Jackson's heart slowed. They weren't talking about him. They were talking about the horse. Still, Brig's gaze remained on him.

"He's too young for arthritis," said Scout, waving a dismissive hand at Brig's diagnosis.

Jackson wanted to tell them that age had nothing to do with joint pain. If an animal was overworked or had direct impact with a joint, pain could exist. And worse, if he was a stubborn male who relied on his strength and prowess, he wouldn't want his weaknesses on display.

His gaze caught Brig's again. It was as though she was reading his mind. But then her blue gaze clouded over, and the mischief was back.

"Pain isn't always obvious," she said. "Sometimes it's in the mind."

Jackson frowned. "You think people fake their pain?"

"Not fake," she said. "Ignore."

It felt like they were having a conversation that wasn't about the horse. But she couldn't know about his knee. The other men didn't know the extent of his injury. If he was lucky, they never would, and he would be past it soon.

Jackson had hit a brick wall with the VA hospital. They gave him only two options; more pain meds or surgery. Neither was his preference. Which was why he'd made an appointment with the university medical center this Monday morning. Hopefully, this Occupational Therapy doctor at the university would have some new treatments for him that would make him as good as new without doping him up or coming at him with a knife.

"I think people often deny what they know to be true because of social acceptance," Brig was saying. "The horse knows he's supposed to work, so he does."

Brig leaned back against the railing. She and Jackson were feet away, but he swore he could feel everywhere her gaze landed on him. It felt like a burst of sunshine. Every word she said was a cool breeze as it reached his ears. Jackson shifted his weight. Unfortunately, he shifted it to his right knee instead of his left. Those penetrating blue eyes caught his wince.

"You know, Scout," said Saylor, "Colonel Brandon is favoring his right leg."

Scout rounded the horse to peer down at his

long legs. Sure enough, every few seconds, he shifted his weight.

"Now that I'm thinking about it, he was stiff when I took him out," said Scout.

"Maybe it is arthritis?" said Saylor.

Saylor said it to Scout as though it was the first time either of them had considered it. Jackson looked to Brig. She shrugged as if the credit passing by her was no big deal.

"I didn't know horses could get arthritis," said Jackson.

"Just because they're big and strong doesn't mean they don't have weaknesses," Brig said as she took one and then another step toward him.

Jackson held still, certain any sudden moves would irritate his knee and give him away. "How do you treat it?"

Brig opened her mouth. But Scout cut her off. Jackson wanted to tell the other woman to keep quiet so he could listen to Brig. But he said nothing.

"Simplest way is to treat it with drugs," said Scout as she scratched behind Colonel Brandon's ear. The horse whinnied and moved away from her touch as though he didn't like the suggestion.

Jackson could relate. Drugs would likely make the horse slower and foggy. He was sure all the animal wanted was to run wild and free like when he was a calf.

"There are other ways to treat stiff joints," said Brig. "If you want to take a walk, I could tell you about some."

Jackson gave himself a shake. He wasn't sure if he'd heard her correctly. Those suggestive words should not come out of a mouth so young and inno-cent. Though standing before him with long legs like a colt and a lush mane of hair, Brigadear Silver looked anything but young and innocent.

"Actually, I did want to talk with you," he said. "I wanted to talk to you all about Gunny."

cold, steel ball clocked Brig in the face. Metaphorically speaking. Miley Cyrus's song *Wrecking Ball* blared in her mind when Jackson mentioned her sister.

She and Jackson had just shared a moment. She knew she wasn't making it up in her mind. His nostrils had flared when she'd talked about his joints. His gaze had widened when she'd suggested they go off alone together. He felt something between the two of them. He was just too fool-headed to admit it.

She'd found that most men were. Her soccer coach had been. Coach Olly had assured Brig that her feelings for him were nothing more than a teenage infatuation. He'd insisted it was pretty common. Although all the other girls on the team had been into the Portuguese phenom Cristiano Ronaldo and seethed at Coach Olly's daily two-hour drills.

Her psychology professor had said the same words in her freshmen year at the university. Though Professor Whitman had named it. Gerontophilia was a condition where someone was attracted to the elderly.

Brig knew that wasn't her jam. She simply preferred her men tall, dark, capable, and with a touch of gray at the temples. Okay, so she might have a thing for older guys. But it wasn't like she trolled old folks' homes.

The boys her age could never hold her attention for long. All they cared about was video games, sports games, and seeing who could get the most phone numbers from girls. Not that they'd even use the numbers to have an actual conversation with the opposite sex. It was all about grammatically incorrect text messages, DMs, and PMs.

Brig had a mind that needed stimulation. Jackson got her synapses firing.

She liked how he looked out for his teammates. She and her sisters were the same way. Though her sisters rarely let her look out for them. So Brig had to do it sneakily. They never thought she had the answers, which was why she didn't take offense when they so quickly discarded her diagnosis of Colonel Brandon.

She had been right about the horse. Brig was often right. It wasn't hard when she lived with opinionated women who often shouted the answers out of turn. Brig always had time to sit back, evaluate all sides, and come to the best conclusion. By that time, her sisters were usually too riled up to listen to reason. So she whispered in their ears, playing mischief and cracking jokes until they thought the idea she insinuated was their own.

It was textbook reverse psychology take that Professor Whitman. See, she had been paying attention. Only the reverse psychology wasn't working on Jackson. And by not working, she meant she was having trouble showing the opposite of her feelings for him.

It always happened this way with a guy she liked. She'd try to play it cool and inevitably wound up throwing herself at him. Well, not this time.

"What do you want to know about Gunny?" she asked Jackson.

Jackson's gaze roved back to hers. He tugged at his lower lip as he looked down at her. That lip made her think of the berries that would soon be in bloom in the north pasture. Brig was suddenly very, very thirsty for some fruit juice.

"What's Gunny like?" he asked.

It was such a simple question. Brig could talk about her sisters for hours. And not just the surface-level stuff. Brig had liked psychology so much that she'd minored in the field. With a family as dysfunctional as hers, it was inevitable that she'd take an interest. Her parents and her sisters were a fascinating lot that could fill volumes of academic texts.

Scout with her control issues. Saylor with her care-taker needs. Aside from being guilt-ridden over the divorce, Mareen's mother had truly screwed up her self-worth. The twins, Tilly and Gunny, had lost their mother shortly after childbirth and had a whole host of abandonment issues. And don't get her started on the daddy issues all of them exhibited. Brig said none of that to Jackson.

"Gunny snores."

Jackson quirked a brow at that. Just another feat most frat boys couldn't manage. On them, the raised brow would look sleazy. On Jackson, it looked devilish.

"She's a cover hog, and she kicks," Brig continued. "I know from experience."

"So, do you," said Scout as she came up to the fence.

"I do not," Brig huffed. Then she moved in front of Scout, hoping that her body blocked out her older sister from Jackson's view.

It might have blocked Scout's face. Unfortunately, it did not block her mouth. "You wet the bed until you were six."

Brig turned and lunged for her sister. The wooden fence that stood in between them was the only thing that saved Scout. That and her cat-like reflexes that had her jumping just beyond Brig's reach.

Brig's cheeks were hotter than red clay in the summer heat. She hesitated to glance up at Jackson. But she couldn't help herself. She was drawn to him. When she looked over, she saw that he was grinning as he looked between the sisters.

Brig was not amused. The man she wanted to marry was looking at her like she was a pampers-soaking, bed-wetting, cover hog who kicked.

"You hear from Gunny?" asked Scout, her attention turning to Jackson. "How's it going with you two?"

"Nothing other than the first email that she'd be here in a few weeks."

A few weeks. That was all the time Brig had to convince Jackson that he was the one for her and not Gunny. Definitely not Gunny, who would prefer to trot the globe saving every endangered animal known to mankind. Jackson needed a woman to look after him, to stand by him, especially with whatever was going on with his knee.

He didn't speak of it, but Brig knew the signs. Horses and men weren't so different.

Unlike the man standing stoically next to Brig, Colonel Brandon took that moment to rear. He wasn't the only one. A few of the other horses who had been sedately eating their morning hay moved around in agitation.

"What's gotten into them?" asked Scout.

"Probably a storm coming," said Brig. Animals could sense changes in weather more accurately than meteorologists.

"Didn't you say you had to go into town?" Scout asked, coming closer to Brig now that the subject of embarrassing childhood stories had passed. Too bad her sister was still smart enough to stay just beyond her reach.

"Yeah, I won't be long," said Brig.

"Your tires were looking a little bald last time I checked."

"I'll get them changed, mom," Brig mocked.

"That would mean you'd have to stay twice as long," said Scout.

"I'm headed into town," said Jackson.

He looked torn as he said it. It was as though the chivalrous knight wanted to care for the damsel. But on the other side, the hardened warrior sensed danger.

See, intelligence. It was so sexy on a man. And it mostly only showed up in the grown variety. Who could truly blame Brig for being attracted to him?

It likely only took a second. To Brig, it looked like the internal battle had waged for years. Finally, the dust settled, and the outcome was announced.

"I can give her a lift."

Perfect. Things were going exactly as she'd planned.

CHAPTER FIVE

ackson winced as he folded himself into the car. As his right knee bent so that his foot could move to its place near the gas pedal, the synovial fluids in the joint released. The resulting sound was similar to a Fourth of July fireworks display.

"I can drive if you'd like," said Brig.

She sat perched at the edge of the passenger seat. The hem of her dress rested just above her knees, which were pressed together primly. A flush of pink colored her perfectly rounded knee caps. She had a dimple in her left knee that mirrored the one that often made an appearance on her left cheek when that mischievous grin slid across her face. Her cheeks blushed that same rosy shade when she was up to something.

Jackson realized he was staring at her knees. He slammed the driver's side door, jammed the key in the ignition, and started the engine. The radio came to life. Miley Cyrus's voice filled the interior like a wrecking ball.

"I love this song," said Brig.

She reached over the armrest that separated them. Jackson tensed, readying to hop out the window. In hindsight, he doubted he would've laughed at his reaction. Having this slip of a girl who all of a sudden looked like a grown woman encroach on his territory would start a war. Scout Silver was not an adversary Jackson wanted or needed. Looking like he was putting the moves on her baby sister when he was all but engaged to a different sister would easily bring on her battle cry.

Brig didn't cross the invisible line between them. She reached instead for the knobs on the radio. With a flick of her wrist, she turned the volume up.

"I was a huge Hannah Montana fan as a kid."

Jackson wanted to tell her that she was still a kid. Those long legs tapping to the beat begged to differ. Why hadn't he told her to put some clothes on before allowing her to hop in the car with him?

Instead of admonishing her state of undress, he said, "I thought this was Miley Cyrus? Who's Hannah Montana?"

"Hannah Montana is Miley Cyrus," she grinned as her head bopped side to side in time to the beat. Then she shimmied her shoulders, which would draw any red-blooded man's attention to her chest.

Jackson thought of ice. He thought of polar bears in the Arctic. His mind went to the poster in Gunny's cabin where a mama polar bear and a baby polar bear walked on thin ice.

That did the trick.

With his libido under control, Jackson pulled out of the long, gravel drive and headed toward the road that would take them to the city. Miley-Hannah crooned on in a country drawl on the two-lane main road that would take them into the highway.

"It was a Disney show that Miley starred in."

Jackson's attention snapped back to the woman beside him. He hadn't noticed the song had finished. Brig was turning down the volume as she spoke. Jackson had no idea what she was talking about.

"The show was called *Hannah Montana*. Miley played the famous singer Hannah Montana, but she wore a wig so she could disguise herself so she could have a normal life as Miley at home."

"Like Jerrica Benton in *Jem and the Holograms?*"

"Who?"

Jackson clamped his mouth shut instead of describing the eighties cartoon his older sister had loved. Though on second thought, maybe he should speak up. He needed to remind them both of their age gap.

"Anyway, I liked the show because I can understand the need to pretend to be something you're not," Brig went on. "Especially when you're trying to protect others."

Jackson glanced at her. Once again, the childish mischief was replaced with clear, blue wisdom. There was more to Brigadear Silver than met the eye. It was something Jackson was not going to uncover.

"How's it going with Carter?" he said, cutting off the radio.

Brig snorted. "Ask Tilly."

Carter and Tilly were spending a lot of time together. More time than the engaged man was spending with the woman he'd agreed to fake marry. Jackson knew nothing inappropriate was going on between Carter and Tilly. In fact, if they all didn't need Carter to marry Brig, then Jackson would've encouraged the bond with Tilly to grow. Carter's attention to the blonde Silver sister was keeping his mind off his other vices.

Where Jackson refused to allow the medication that dulled his pain to become his master, Carter had long ago bent the knee. Metaphorically, speaking. Jackson couldn't blame the man. Combat was ugly and left deep wounds that didn't always heal, especially the internal ones.

"Carter's a good guy," said Jackson.

"He'd better be if he's going to marry my sister," said Brig.

"He's going to marry you."

"Wanna make a bet?" Brig cocked a brow, part question mark, part challenge.

Also, the mischief was back in that clear blue gaze. That was good. Jackson was better with the mischief than with the clarity and wisdom.

"I knew Scout and Linc would tie the knot that first day. They're both used to being in charge, so it made sense that they would join forces. Like Saylor, Jeff is a peacemaker—so that was inevitable. Mareen and Wilson both feel like outsiders, even though they are loved by the people who care about them."

Jackson snuck another glance at Brig in his peripheral vision. Once again, the mischief was gone from her gaze. It was replaced by a light of wisdom that was far beyond her two decades of living. She looked older than her twenty years.

"It took a little while to realize that Tilly and Carter were going to be a thing since they keep talking about the other guys she's dating," Brig continued to muse. "But they're both codependent. As a twin, Tilly's not used to being on her own. She'll never admit it, but when Gunny left to travel, it hit her hard."

Brig turned that blue gaze on him. Jackson felt she saw right through him. Her perceptions thus far were dead on. He didn't need her looking more deeply into him.

"You think Carter's codependent?" he said.

"I do," she said. "But I don't think it's another person he needs. I can't put my finger on it yet. But it's clear to me he and Tilly need each other more than he needs me. I'm not going to hold still and talk about eighties fashion wrecks."

"Hey, don't knock the eighties."

"Why not? You weren't born yet."

"I was born before this century began."

"So was I," said Brig. "I was born in 1999. You were born, what? 1990?"

That was the year of his birth. That gave them a nine-year age gap, not the ten he'd assumed. Still, it was an age gap. Jackson merged onto the highway, but he stayed in the slow lane.

"Truman is like a wounded animal," Brig went on. "Gunny is great with wounded animals."

"I'm marrying Gunny."

Brig turned to him with a wicked smile, but those blue eyes were clear. Clear and serious. "No. You're not."

It sounded worse than a threat. It sounded like a promise.

A horn blared, yanking Jackson's attention back to the road. He straightened the wheel just in time. He'd swerved over into a faster lane. But he hadn't picked up the pace.

"You sure you don't want me to take the wheel?" said Brig. "You drive like an old fuddy-duddy."

"I'm fine." His voice came out more harshly than he'd meant it to.

"Okay, Boomer."

"Boomer? How old do you think I am?"

"Not as old as *you* think you are."

Brig turned the radio back on. It was a Cyrus kind of afternoon. Miley's dad was crooning *Achy Breaky Heart.*

They drove the rest of the way without conversation. But Jackson's mind stayed on Brig. She relaxed next to him in the passenger seat, even closing her eyes as she hummed along to the music. She was completely trusting of him. Little did she know that he wanted to pull over and...

And what? Finally, learn what that mischievous grin tasted like? He couldn't do that. She was a child. He had to keep reminding himself of that. Except that in the conversation he'd had with her, Brig proved she might be the baby of the family in age, but not in intellect.

So why did she act so immature when there were flashes of what could only be called brilliance and insight in those blue eyes? She might think Gunny wasn't the one for him, but Jackson knew Brig could never be that woman.

CHAPTER SIX

"I'll drop you where you need to go," said Jackson.

Brig opened her eyes as the car came down to a slower speed. She was a sucker for falling asleep on long car rides. She hadn't fallen asleep just now. She'd just felt so relaxed, so right being near Jackson Bennett that she'd let her eyes close and her guard down.

"Here's good," she said, yawning. She stretched her arms over her head and arched her back to work out the stiff spot there. When she turned, she found Jackson's gaze latched on her form.

Not exactly on her face. His eyes roved from her arms over her head, down to the curve of her elbow, and finally at her raised chest.

He didn't avert his gaze as she unfurled her body and pressed her back against the cushion of the passenger seat. He had yet to blink when her arms slowly came down from over her head to rest in her lap.

Jackson was attracted to her. Even more, he wanted her. Which was just fine with Brig because she wanted him right back.

Call it gerontophilia. She didn't care. That touch of gray at his temples did something to her belly, and she wasn't ashamed. Jackson's cheekbones were starker than Cristiano Ronaldo's could've ever hoped to be. If Jackson stepped out on a soccer field, he'd win World Cups just with a grin.

He wasn't grinning at her. His eyes widened with guilt when he saw he'd been caught.

He sure was caught. Soon he'd be tied up in a nice little bow if she had her way, and Brig usually did. She'd laid hint after hint that she was a full-grown woman. Finally, the idea was taking root in that thick skull of his.

Surprisingly, manipulating a grown man was harder than it was with her sisters.

Jackson put the car in park. As soon as he cut the engine, he hopped out of the vehicle as though it were on fire.

Brig waited patiently in her seat like her father had taught her. More times than not, when she'd gone out on dates with boys her age, she found herself waiting long after they'd walked away from the car.

Not Jackson. After a slow exhale and a shake of his head, he rounded the car and opened the passenger door for her. Brig held out her hand. Jackson didn't hesitate to offer his own in assistance.

The moment their fingers touched, that guilty expression clouded his vision again. He dropped her hand like it was on fire. But he kept it hovering at her low back until they were both out of the street and on the sidewalk. Then he turned to face her.

"I'm not sure how long my appointment will be," he said. "I'll text you when I'm done."

"You can't. You don't have my number."

Jackson handed her his phone. Brig tapped into his contacts, adding her own. When she handed the phone back to Jackson, he smirked at what she'd written there.

"Brigalicious?"

She gave him a wink.

He tried and failed to wipe the grin off his face. "I'll see you in a bit."

It was a warm day with the sun shading itself

behind a few clouds. Coeds were out on blankets with books and tablets. A few guys played ultimate frisbee on the lawn. Midterms had passed a couple of weeks ago, and the workload wasn't yet heavy with finals a couple of months away.

Brig didn't have many academic classes left. She'd finished all the classroom requirements of her degree over a year ago. All of her remaining course-work was practical and hands-on.

Jackson turned to walk into the university clinic. Brig trailed behind him. He looked over his shoulder, giving her a quizzical expression. "Don't you have to get to class?"

"This is my classroom," she said, pointing to the clinic.

Jackson's expression morphed from questioning to wary. Brig stepped up to the closed glass doors. She lifted her gaze to Jackson expectantly. The gentleman in him took over and opened the door.

"Hey, sweetie," said the receptionist, with a deep Southern twang.

Brig hated to be called by sugary endearments. Today's college women had a habit of calling each other *babe* and *sweets*. It turned her stomach as though she'd eaten a bunch of Valentine Sweet Tarts. But when Ronnie Mae Barton, with her cloud of gray curls and her kind pale eyes, called her sweetie, Brig couldn't muster the ire to mind. So maybe she did have a touch of gerontophilia.

"Hi, Mrs. Barton. How are you today?"

"My old bones are aching," she said. "Must mean a storm is coming."

Brig smiled at the old superstition. The weatherman had called for sunny skies all week. Outside, there wasn't a cloud in the sky.

"Good morning, sir," Ronnie Mae said, turning her attention to Jackson. "Can you sign in here please?"

Jackson picked up the pen and began the paperwork.

"Brig, sweetie, before you go Dr. Vargas wanted to know if you'd consult with her on a new patient," said the receptionist.

Brig nodded with as much nonchalance as she could muster. That consult, which she'd seen on the books when she was here last week, was her only pretense for being in the clinic today. All of her files were up to date. All of her paperwork in order.

"There's been a lot of job offers for you," Ronnie continued. "Have you made your decision on where you'll go after graduation?"

Brig still had a year left in her program. She'd

been interning and volunteering in clinics all over the state for the last three years, aiming to learn all the best techniques. Now that she had them, there was only one place she'd ever take them.

"You know I'm gonna work on my family ranch," said Brig. "But I'll always be happy to consult at the clinic after graduation."

Brig caught Jackson glancing at her from his paperwork. He hadn't gotten past the first question, which was Patient's Last Name.

"Dr. Vargas, your next appointment is here," Ronnie Mae said to the petite brunette coming into the waiting area.

"Mr. Bennett?"

Jackson dropped the pen to shake Dr. Vargas's hand.

"And Brig, you're here too. I was hoping you'd consult on this case."

Jackson's gaze went wide. Wider than when he'd been caught gazing at her arched back. He opened his mouth as though ready to form a protest.

"Ms. Silver is my best student in Occupational Therapy," Dr. Vargas was saying. "Not just in this year's class, but ever. I put a lot of weight on her expertise."

"I'll be happy to sit in," said Brig. "If Mr. Bennett is open to hearing my advice."

Jackson looked at Brig as though she was a stranger. Brig was uncertain if her little game had been the best move. But what other move did she have? Before this, he hadn't seen her as the grown, capable woman she was. In this capacity, he'd have to.

CHAPTER SEVEN

Jackson sat on a hospital gurney. He had his shirt on, a pair of boxer briefs, and a paper-thin hospital gown. A slight chill ran through the room, but that's not what made him into a ball of tension.

"This all began with a torn meniscus?" asked Dr. Vargas.

The woman was pretty, average height, and curvy in all the right places. In her mid-thirties if Jackson ventured a guess. Not that he'd ever say so out loud. His mama didn't raise a fool who'd ask women about their age or their weight.

Still, a fool he was as he looked past Dr. Vargas and to the woman standing behind her. Brig now donned a white doctor's coat. Thankfully, that addition to her wardrobe enhanced the straight lines of her body, making her look like a young girl playing doctor. Somehow Jackson still found that adorable.

So not only did he have a thing for young girls, now he was hot for doctors? No, not doctors in the plural. Just this one doctor.

Wait? Was Brig an actual doctor? She couldn't be? She was too young.

"I tore my meniscus last year," said Jackson. "It was after an impact blast."

Brig looked out the window. She closed her eyes and exhaled. When she turned back, she caught Jackson's gaze. She knew what that impact blast had been. It had been the blast that had killed her father. Jackson had walked away with a limp. General Silver hadn't walked away at all.

Jackson held the gaze of the General's youngest daughter. Her eyes were the exact same shade as his. Her chin tilted high, just as proudly as her father's. Jackson worried that his mention of the incident had upset her. He should've known better. Brig was every bit her father's daughter. She nodded as if giving him permission to go on.

"A year before that," Jackson continued once he knew Brig was going to be all right, "I had a ligament tear. And five years ago, I fractured it."

"All on the same knee?" asked Dr. Vargas.

Jackson nodded.

Dr. Vargas pursed her lips. She flipped through a few pages on the chart. Then she tapped her pen at her lips.

Jackson should have noticed how lush her lips were. He should've thought about kissing those lips. Instead, he fought to stare at Dr. Vargas instead of doing what he really wanted to do, which was to lift his gaze and check on Brig.

"What's your diagnosis, Ms. Silver?"

Brig inhaled slowly, her gaze never wavering from Jackson's. There again, he spied the light of wisdom in those clear blue eyes. "Osteoarthritis."

"What?" The single word was harsh when it came out of Jackson's mouth. "Isn't that what old people get?"

"You'll be what? Thirty this year. That's getting up there, buddy."

Brig's tone was mocking. Jackson knew that even though she said *buddy,* what she was thinking was *boomer.* The jab should've stung. Because it was their private joke, it spread warmth through him.

"I take it you two know each other?" said Dr. Vargas peering between both of them.

"Mr. Bennett is staying on my family's ranch.

Watching him these past few weeks, I noticed that the pain is usually in the mornings. He appears to go on a brisk walk at dawn to warm the joint up. I've noticed his walks going slightly longer recently, which indicates that the pain is progressing."

Jackson stared, dumbfounded. He hadn't even known that anyone was watching him on his morning walks. To hear how detailed Brig described his daily habits made him feel as though he'd been under surveillance. The woman would've been perfect for the intel division of the military.

"The joint is swelling now," Brig said as she bent down to peer at his bare leg. "There have been times when I've heard the popping of joint noise, all which tell me it's progressing."

Dr. Vargas nodded. Jackson felt like a lab rat as he sat between the two women who spoke about him as though he wasn't cognizant.

"What would your treatment plan be?" asked Dr. Vargas.

Brig turned from the doctor and looked directly at Jackson. "I know he did equine therapy at a reha-bilitation ranch for veterans. It's clear that has been beneficial. I think he needs to stay that course at Silver Star. He could stay on the Fentanyl that the military prescribed, but I don't think it necessary. I think with the physical activity of riding, with added physical therapy, Mr. Bennett could be put on an aspirin regimen."

Jackson's lips parted as he looked at this woman. There wasn't a hint of mischief in Brig's gaze. He sat there under the full brunt of those intelligent blue eyes. He felt seen in the darkness that had surrounded him this past year. He felt heard, even though he hadn't spoken of his pain. His hands itched to pull her close. And then she came closer.

When her fingertips touched his knee, Jackson kicked out in reflex. Luckily, Brig moved to the side. Jackson's toes caught Dr. Vargas's charts, and the clipboard went flying.

"Sorry," said Jackson.

"No worries," said Dr. Vargas. "It's just papers."

"It's my fault," said Brig. "I should've warned you I was going to touch you. Jackson?"

"Yes, Brig."

"I'm going to touch you."

The thoughts that went through Jackson's mind at that phrase were not Disney friendly. He sat still as Brig's hand landed on his knee. Her gaze was all cool assessment as she poked and prodded his knee as countless medical professionals had done over the years.

Brig was different. Her hands on him felt right. Her proximity to him felt inevitable. He hadn't known he was in a battle until he realized he'd lost.

Brig wanted him. Of that, he was sure. Now he was also sure that she was going to have him. She was going to win this entire war if he didn't do something soon.

"Dr. Vargas." The gray-haired receptionist poked her head in the door. "I'm sorry to interrupt, but you have an urgent call."

"Excellent work, Brig. I agree with all of your recommendations. Will you finish up this chart and answer any of Mr. Bennett's questions? I'll be back to finish up once I'm done with my call."

"Sure thing," said Brig.

She took the chart and pen. The doctor and receptionist went out the door. The door closed with a quiet snick. Then it was just the two of them.

All Jackson could hear in the room was the *scratch scratch* of Brig's pen as she made notes on the documents. She didn't look up at him when she spoke.

"Do you have any questions for me, Mr. Bennett?"

"How long have you been watching me?"

She still didn't look up. But the corner of her lip

quirked into that mischievous grin. "Since the day you stepped out of that truck and winced when your right foot hit the ground."

Jackson blew the breath he was holding out his nose. He emptied out his lungs and chest. Then he took a new breath and made one last attempt to win this battle between them.

"You can't treat me," he said.

"You don't think I know what I'm doing?"

Her face fell. No mischief. No intelligence. There was only hurt.

"It's clear you know exactly what you're doing, Brigadear. In more ways than one."

Brig sat the paperwork on the counter and took a step toward him. Jackson had the inclination to back down, but he knew better than to show his enemy his neck.

That thought brought his gaze to Brig's neck. It was long and slender. He wondered if she'd taste salty or sweet? She'd probably be all spice and fireworks.

"Jackson..." Brig reached for him.

Jackson held still, waiting for those fingers to impact him. He was uncertain what he'd do when they did. He was uncertain what his response would be to her words.

He needn't have worried. Before Brig's hands could reach his flesh or her words reach his ears, the entire room shook. He felt the earth move under his feet. He heard a large groan that sounded inhuman.

Jackson reached for Brig as the world went off-kilter. He brought her into his arms, sheltering her with his body, caring not for his injuries, only trying to protect her from harm as the world shook all around them.

CHAPTER EIGHT

"I've got you, baby."

The earth had literally moved, shifting Brig into exactly the place she wanted to be. She was cradled in Jackson's strong arms. She was tucked snuggly into his chest. One of his hands spanned her small back, clutching her to him. The other nestled her head into the crook of his neck. His palm was the softest, warmest cushion she'd ever come in contact with. She didn't know how she'd fall asleep ever again without it. She also knew she could never sleep if she found herself in this position.

Jackson's gaze wasn't on her. It was flitting about the room. The warrior part of him was clear in his hazel eyes. He assessed the threat to the both of them as he used his body as protection against hers.

As far as Brig was concerned, there was no threat, only fate. All of her scheming over the last couple of weeks had nothing on the power of Mother Nature. And because Mother Nature had intervened when Brig needed a miracle, it was more proof that she and Jackson were meant to be.

"It was an earthquake," Brig said. Her tone was calm because she'd grown up in Montana. Most people looked at California for its earth-shattering records, but Montana had its fair share of seismic activity each year.

Jackson's face came back to hers. He peered down at her as though just remembering that she was there. His gaze dipped to her lips.

Brig licked her lips and moistened her bottom lip. Jackson tracked the movement. His nostrils flared, a hunger in his eyes.

Brig didn't have a lot of experience with the opposite sex. She'd had no patience for the fumbling of the boys her age when they'd tried to grope her. The grown men she had been interested in had always kept at least six feet of distance between them at all times. This was the first time Brig had been in the embrace of a man she wanted to hold her.

She wasn't sure how to get him to come closer. So she did what any Silver daughter would do. She took command.

Brig lifted her head to meet Jackson's lips. The soldier in him was all reflex. He jerked back out of her reach without letting go of his protective hold. When he did so, he let out a sharp gasp of pain.

It must have been the pain that caused him to release her. Jackson rolled off her. He let her go and clutched at his knee.

Oh, no. His knee. Had he injured it more?

Brig scrambled to her own knees to get a better look. There was no blood. Just a dark flush on his brown skin where the wrinkle of his knee cap sat.

"Don't try to stand," Brig ordered. "Stay there. You need to rest it."

Jackson pried his eyes open. In those hazel depths, Brig heard the message loud and clear. It fairly shouted, *you think?*

Men in pain made for the worst patients. Brig went to the fridge, picking her way over debris left by the shaking earth. The door to the mini-fridge was open. She reached in and grabbed an ice pack.

Jackson hissed when she put the bag on his knee. Brig wouldn't have been surprised if he started wailing like a baby, like many of the other males that came into this clinic. She should've known better. After the initial harsh breath, Jackson pressed his lips together and focused on his breathing through his nose.

"I want to bandage it, to add compression."

The moment she touched his skin, he hissed again. Her gaze darted to his. She knew she couldn't have hurt him. She hadn't touched the knee, just the space above his thigh.

Then Brig realized that wasn't pain twisting his lips now. It hadn't been the first time either. It was a flare of desire, desire Jackson was trying to hide from her.

"Don't be a baby," she chided.

"Don't be a child," he struck back.

"I'm a grown woman. Did you know that I'll be twenty-one in a matter of months?"

Jackson's brows rose, giving her another glimpse of the interest he was trying desperately to hide. Brig didn't clarify that the matter wouldn't happen for nearly nine months.

"You're in my care," she said. "Which means you need to listen to me."

"I'm supposed to be protecting you," he said as

she carefully wrapped the tan adhesive around his knee. "It's what I promised your father; that I'd look after all of you."

"My dad raised six capable women. I'm starting to believe he wanted us to look after the six of you more than he wanted you to look after us."

A small smile tugged at his lips. The mention of the general hailed a temporary truce between them. Jackson's posture relaxed as he leaned back against the wall. Brig curled her knees under her as she scooted closer to him to finish tying the bandage.

He winced again as she tied the end of the knot. "You need to work on your bedside manner."

"Happy to. Once I get you in bed."

Jackson's nostrils flared again before he tamped it down. Brig grinned triumphantly. He could deny all he wanted that she wasn't having an effect on him.

She cocked her head toward the gurney, eyes full of an innocence that neither of them bought. Jackson moved to get up, wincing as he did so. Brig put her arms around him.

"I've got this," he said.

"Now who's acting like a child?" she said. "Lean on me."

The set to his jaw was stubborn. "Don't you

know soldiers have a hard time showing vulnerability?"

"I'm good at fixing broken things," she said. "There's a part of you that's broken. Let me fix it."

That changed his features. He didn't look relaxed. He didn't look tense. The only word that Brig could find to describe how Jackson looked down at her was resigned. She wasn't sure if that was a good thing?

He put an arm around her but didn't give her any of his weight. He winced again as they rose to stand. Brig had to brace herself against the wall to take on his weight. When she did, she realized it was her back against the wall as he loomed over her.

Jackson had her pinned against the wall. His arms boxed her in. His breathing became shallow. A bead of sweat formed on his brow.

Brig reached up and wiped it away. Jackson didn't track her movements. His gaze was fixed on her mouth once more. That's when she knew that resignation was a good thing.

Jackson wasn't giving up. He was giving in.

CHAPTER NINE

*J*ackson hadn't noticed the pain when he'd been holding Brig in his arms, protecting her on the ground after the quake. He'd forgotten the pain while he had her caged against the wall, her lips so close to his.

He might have been the injured party, but there was no way she could escape him. He had her well and trapped. Then a brief moment of clarity struck him when he looked into those clear blue.

Brigadear Silver wasn't trapped. She was exactly where she wanted to be. Jackson was the one with no escape.

He was going to kiss her. There was no other choice. Once he kissed her, his path would be set. He would have to marry her. Spend the rest of his days with her. Raise children with her, children with clear blue eyes and caramel-colored skin who would wreak havoc up and down the valley with their mother's penchant for mischief and his military prowess.

The world was doomed.

A loud boom sounded from the other side of the door. Jackson pulled Brig against his chest, tucking her forehead against his neck to ensure he would bear any of the brunt of the oncoming attack. She fit perfectly into the contours of his body like they were parts of a puzzle that had been pulled apart a long time ago. Now that they were back together, the frayed edges of his person felt whole.

"Brig? Mr. Bennett? Are you okay in there?"

The pounding sounded again. The rational part of Jackson knew the person on the other side of the door wasn't a threat. Still, he couldn't make his hands let Brig go. She was no help. She'd wrapped her arms around his waist and held fast.

"We're fine," she said into his chest.

"The door's jammed. Hold on, we're going to get you out."

Jackson wanted to roar at whoever was on the other side of that door. Didn't they hear Brig? The two of them were just fine the way they were.

There was a vibrant, beautiful woman in his arms. A woman looking up at him with the same desire he felt for her. It burned so hot between them that it dulled the ache in his knee. The only pain Jackson felt was the burning in his belly to claim Brig.

With brute force, the door opened. The doctor, the receptionist, and a burly security guard looked at the two of them. Their surprised looks were what finally snapped Jackson out of the dream world and back to reality.

Jackson had Brig pinned against the wall. He stood there in a shirt and his boxers and nothing else. The hospital gown had ripped off him at some point during the earthquake.

This was entirely improper.

But why?

Because he was a patient, and Brig was his doctor? No, that wasn't it.

"You okay, sweetie?" asked the receptionist.

Sweetie? The endearment that came from the gray-haired woman seemed meant for a child. Then Jackson remembered; Brig was a child. Though his brain rejected that notion as he looked down at her.

"We're fine," Brig answered.

She took a step past him. Jackson hesitated to let

her go. The moment she left his hold, the pain in his knee slammed back into him. He knew she hadn't used an ounce of her strength to hold him up. He'd been the one holding her. Still, the moment she left his side, he couldn't hold on any longer, and he slumped against the wall.

Brig turned back to him. Concern etched in her pretty features. Jackson didn't like the look in her eyes. It was neither mischievous nor knowing. She looked scared.

He reached out for her, but he missed. He had a couple of inches on Brig in height, but she seemed to be growing taller with each passing second. All the while, the look in her blue eyes grew darker as her gaze widened. She was supposed to look at him as though he hung the moon. But she looked at him as though he was a sinking ship.

Because he was sinking. He was slowly going to the ground.

"He re-injured himself protecting me," she said as she crouched over him. "I bandaged the knee and had started applying ice."

"Good work, Brig," said Dr. Vargas. Her blunt fingers inspected the work at his knee. "Looks like you had a bit of excitement today, Mr. Bennet.

Earthquakes are unpredictable. But Montana has its fair share of them. Luckily that one wasn't so bad."

Wasn't so bad? It had knocked Jackson off his feet. It had made him appear vulnerable and weak to Brig. That boom of the earth shaking had rattled his bones, making him feel like the Boomer Brig had accused him of being.

"Nothing's broken," said the doctor after an examination. "Just get him back to the ranch and start your course of therapy."

This was said to Brig. Jackson expected the mischievous grin to make an appearance. What made him quake in his bones was that Brig didn't grin at him. She looked at him with that clear blue gaze that unnerved him. That gaze unnerved him because it always made her look older than her nearly twenty-one years. It made her appear like she wasn't just on par with him age-wise; it made him feel like she was more than his equal. It made him feel like she was about to conquer him.

"Y ou feeling better today, big boy?"

In response, the big boy in question dipped its head and snagged the apple out of Brig's palm. If only all men could be bought so easily.

Brig looked over her shoulder at Gunny's cabin. The front door hadn't opened yet today. It probably wouldn't since Jackson had been given orders by Dr. Vargas to rest his leg today after yesterday's natural disaster.

The worse the quake had done on the ranch was knock some of the tack off the walls in the barns and portraits in the houses. The main house and the cabins were all built to withstand a quake. Not to mention, the animals often gave a fair warning when something out of the ordinary was about to occur.

"We just weren't paying attention to you yesterday, were we, boy?"

Colonel Brandon took an unsteady step. He was much more agreeable today now that the ground beneath him was silent and still. Brig might not have paid attention to his behavior about the earthquake, but she was listening to the horse's complaint about his joints.

"Don't worry, buddy. We just need to work that leg out. You'll be dancing again with Mareen in no time."

The horse brushed his long nose against the side of Brig's face, much like an affectionate dog would do, only without the slobbering tongue lashing. At least the horse wasn't afraid to show her affection. Unlike some grown men who preferred to hide out in their cabins.

Jackson hadn't even allowed her to drive them home after the quake. He'd sent for Carter and Truman to drive into town to chauffeur them back. Then he'd stuck Brig in the car with Carter while he got into the passenger seat of Truman's truck.

Brig knew it wasn't the earthquake that had shaken Jackson up so much. It was that near kiss.

She'd seen the spark in his eyes. It was easy to recognize since she'd felt it every time she'd looked at him these past couple of weeks.

For a few minutes the other day, Jackson had seen her. Really seen her. Seen her as more than the youngest Silver sister. He'd seen her as a capable, intelligent, desirable woman. And that had rattled him.

She wanted to stomp over there and bang on his door. But that wouldn't be the mature thing to do.

So what should she do? She was done playing the waiting game. They were running out of time.

Colonel Brandon stumbled, bringing them both up to a halt. Brig bent and ran her hand over the horse's front carpus. She breathed a sigh of relief when she didn't find any swelling. The horse held still, allowing her to massage the joint. Another difference between man and beast, the horse didn't kick out when she touched his leg.

Why was Jackson so afraid of what was between them? Was it really the age thing? They weren't that far apart in age. Both of them were in their twenties.

Maybe he had his sights set on Gunny? But he'd never seen Gunny. Brig was pretty sure the two of them had never had a conversation outside of a few lines of emails. Even if they had, she knew that her globe-trotting, save-the-animals sister was not the right woman for Jackson.

Jackson was a family man. He had set-me-down-with-roots written all over him. Brig wasn't ready to be a mother. Not yet. But when the time came, she wanted to be rooted right alongside him, whereas Gunny would never hold still in one place long enough to be caught.

"There you are."

Brig lifted her head at the sound of her sister's voice. Scout was a few yards away, but her voice carried as though she was standing right next to Brig. If Scout had joined the military, their father had hoped, she would've been the scariest drill sergeant that ever barked an order.

Brig never jumped when Scout spoke. Because as harsh as her sister's bite was, her hugs were the most comforting thing in the world. And besides, Brig knew Scout would never order her to do something that would put her in harm's way.

"We need to start talking details about your and Carter's wedding."

"Scouttie," Brig said patiently, "I'm not marrying Carter."

"Of course you are. It's decided."

Usually, Brig didn't mind her sisters trying to

run her life. She was too good at covertly turning them around and steering their directives the way she already wanted to go. "You know Carter's into Tilly?"

"Their friends." Scout's tone was dismissive.

As if they heard their names called, Carter and Tilly came out of the barn. They were laughing and jabbing at each other. It was not inappropriate. They looked like best buddies. But Brig knew being best buddies was often a precursor to romance.

Scout looked at the two of them with a pinched expression as they rounded the barn and headed into the house. Scout opened her mouth as though to yell. Brig knew her sister's voice would easily carry across that distance. But that wasn't the direction Brig wanted to go.

"What if I'm into someone else?" Brig said before Scout could bark any order.

Again, Scout's features squinched into a pinched expression. "That might be for the best."

Scout's brows drew together as her gaze narrowed. Brig turned to peer in the direction of Scout's new focus. Truman walked up to Tilly and Carter. After a few seconds of what looked like a greeting, Carter went off with Truman, though his gaze lingered on Tilly as she walked up the porch steps and into the house.

"Truman's not into it," said Scout.

Brig breathed a sigh of relief. Once again, the right words whispered into her sister's ears were going to get her exactly what she wanted.

"I'll talk him into it," Scout continued. "I'll twist his arm if I have to."

Scout didn't wait around for Brig's next words. She marched off in the direction of the house. Brig didn't bother correcting her sister. Once Scout got on a path, even a path Brig tried to direct her bull-headed sister down, it was hard to steer her until she reached the end.

Everyone in this family thought they knew what was best for Brig. Sometimes they were even right. But not this time. It was crystal clear to Brig that she was going to marry Jackson, whether everyone liked it or not. And that included Jackson.

CHAPTER ELEVEN

*J*ackson could see Brig in the distance, but for once, her gaze was not on him. Her attention was on Colonel Brandon. She patiently walked the arthritic horse around in a slow circle. Even from this distance, Jackson could see the horse's uneven gait as his front right leg gingerly contacted the ground.

This morning, Jackson had had the same reaction when he'd put weight on his right leg. The joints there protested more than normal. Likely because of the impact of his world shifting the day before.

He'd nearly kissed Brig. He'd wanted to with every fiber of his being. Right now, every fiber, even the disjointed ones in his legs, urged him to make his way to her and complete that mission.

Laying in the bed for an entire day, Jackson had felt like he was lying in darkness. Even though the light of the sun had shone through the curtains. The moment he was breathing the same air as Brig, he felt like a switch had been turned on inside him, and he could finally see the dawn.

"You look like hell," said Truman. He leaned against the frame of the cabin next door.

"Survived an earthquake," Jackson shot back.

"You survived bomb blasts and looked better," said Carter.

"Aren't you supposed to be resting those old bones?" said Truman.

Jackson shook his head. "Doc said I needed to walk it a bit the next day."

"Which doctor?" asked Truman, his gaze turning to where Brig walked the horse.

Carter turned too. His eyes lighting up once they landed on the woman in question.

Jackson felt the urge to wring his brother's neck. He couldn't stand to have any man look at Brig as though she was the dessert he was about to dig into. The truth was that Carter had claimed that right. Carter had agreed to marry Brig. Carter would get to indulge in the sweetness of that clever mouth.

The grin on Carter's face fairly shouted that he couldn't wait. But then the clouds in the sky shifted, and Jackson saw that Tilly had joined Brig in the round pen.

An enormous weight lifted off Jackson's shoulders. The sigh of relief that left Jackson's chest was audible. He would've hated to kill one of his best friends. Especially if it had to be Carter. If he'd have had to wring the man's neck, Jackson would've been left with oily gel all over his hands.

"I take it back," said Truman. "You're looking combat-ready all of a sudden."

There was a knowing light in Truman's gaze. The sniper's vision was sharp. Not that it needed to be when Jackson was standing at close range.

Jackson looked away, but not before sneaking another glance at the pen. "I'm gonna work the knee."

"We'll come with you," said Truman.

"I don't need a babysitter."

"Really?" said Truman. "Cause it sounds like you're pitching a fit."

Jackson huffed. Once upon a time, he could outrun both of them. However, with his injury, he knew they could outpace him with nothing more than a fast walk. So, he resigned himself to being followed.

At least they didn't demand he banter with them. Carter could talk to a wall and hold an engaging conversation. Instead of walls, Carter's voice bounced off trees. Leaves rustled in the breezeless afternoon. Branches crunched underfoot.

Truman offered infrequent grunts of his inattentiveness. Jackson remained entirely mute. He was far too lost in his own thoughts to even follow Carter's monologue.

Jackson needed to figure out what he needed to do about Brig. More to the point, his inappropriate desire to kiss the young woman. She might be turning twenty-one in a matter of months, as she'd said. But she was still far too green behind the ears to get mixed up with a man like him.

But if not him, then who? Definitely not Carter. Jackson would never consign Brig to a loveless marriage, even if temporary. It was clear to anyone paying attention that Carter had it bad for Tilly.

Not Truman, either. That soldier had it bad for his old job. Truman was working hard to rehabilitate his shoulder injury. Before shrapnel had lodged in his shooting arm, Truman had been one of the best snipers in the Armed Forces. He had a single-minded determination to get that title back. Meaning there was no woman in his plan. Unless she was standing within the crosshairs of a target.

That left only Jackson.

A hand shot out in front of him. Jackson looked beside him to see Truman with his hand outstretched. His friend's gaze was on the ground. A root rose out of the earth. One more step, and Jackson would've easily caught the tree's overgrown vine. One more fall could easily take his knee out.

"Thanks, man."

Truman nodded wordlessly.

Carter kept babbling on in front of them as though nothing had happened.

Age aside, this was the other reason Jackson could never be the man for Brig. She was young and vibrant. Where his body was already giving up on him before he'd even hit thirty. He could never keep up with her.

The sound of horse hooves came near. Jackson tensed, wondering if it was Brig. Was he hoping it was her? If he was honest, he would admit that he was.

Knowing he wasn't right for her was one thing.

But thinking about how right she felt in his arms was an entirely different matter.

While he lay in bed all day yesterday, all he thought about was her. The feel of her against his chest. The taste of her breath so close to his lips. He'd nearly kissed her, and man, had he wanted to. Still wanted to. Which was why he was putting distance between them.

But if she came to him?

Jackson looked up to see the rider. It wasn't a brown-haired girl. It was a brown-skinned man. Jackson and the two other soldiers immediately stood at attention as Father Matthews rode toward them.

"Afternoon, gentlemen."

"Colonel," they all intoned.

Haran Matthews shook his head at the three stiff soldiers standing in formation. The old man was a decorated war hero with more medals and stars that the three of them had combined. Father Matthews came from a line of decorated war heroes from the Buffalo Soldiers to the Tuskegee Airman. He had been a pilot himself in his youth. Now he contented himself with the care of horses while also keeping a watchful eye on his best friend's six daughters.

"I hear I'll be officiating another wedding soon,"

said Father Matthews, who was also an ordained minister. In fact, he preferred to be called Father Matthews.

Father Matthews' eyes landed on Carter. For once in his life, Carter was momentarily tongue-tied.

"Right," said Carter, finding his voice. "That would be me. I'll be marrying..."

"Brig." Truman supplied for him.

Carter blinked as though he didn't recognize the name.

"That's surprising," said Father Matthews. "With as much as I've seen you and Artillery about town together."

"Oh, no." Carter waved the notion away as though it were a trifling matter. "Tilly and I are just friends."

"And you and Brig?" prompted the pastor.

"Me and Brig?" Carter looked confused. "Oh, yeah, Brig's a great kid."

"She's not a kid."

All eyes swung to Jackson. He stood chewing on his lip as though chastising it for speaking. But the words were the truth.

"Brigadear is a very accomplished young

woman," Jackson managed to say. "And she'll be twenty-one in a matter of months."

"I remember when her father fell for her mother," said Father Matthews. "Did you know he was ten years older than Sarah? Sarah's parents wouldn't hear of the marriage. But Sarah was determined. She threatened to elope if her parents didn't agree."

Jackson was still thinking about Father Matthews's first words before the rest of the pastor's words caught up with him. The general had married a much younger woman? And that woman had been defiant. Seemed Brig and her mother had a lot in common.

"My wife was fifteen years older than me." Father Matthews went on. "I think you boys would call her a cougar? We didn't have any children of our own. We adopted our boys. Love doesn't see age or blood. It just sees a heart like its own."

Father Matthews's gaze landed on Jackson. Those dark eyes seemed to see directly into Jackson's heart. Whatever the general's best friend saw there, it made him smile.

"Let me know about those wedding dates, boys," said the pastor as he directed his horse to walk on. "None of us are getting any younger."

CHAPTER TWELVE

"Come on, twinkle toes. You owe me a dance."

Colonel Brandon got off to a slow start as Brig walked him out of the barn the next morning. She didn't mount him yet, knowing he needed a good warm-up. His movements were sluggish as she led him around the pen. Too bad horses couldn't have canes.

"How's he doing this morning?" asked Mareen.

She and Tilly came inside the pen. Colonel Brandon immediately pulled to go to Mareen. Brig let him go. The colonel's slow start quickly picked up as he made his way to his owner and former dance partner.

As a teenager, Colonel Brandon and Mareen had

taken the dressage stage by storm. The horse was already in his prime when they'd partnered up. All these years later, and the colonel's heart was still aching to move, but his body just wasn't willing. Though the body-mind connection seemed to snap back into place as he high stepped it to Mareen.

Mareen smiled at the horse, giving him a nuzzle and a scratch behind his ears. The simple wedding band on her hand left hand caught in the morning sunlight. The former society miss wore worn jeans and boots instead of her normal tailored dresses and heels. Mareen Silver Michaels looked as young, fresh, happy as the days when she'd dance with Colonel Brandon. That's what love could do for a person; change them inside and out.

"He's doing good this morning," Brig said in answer to her sister's earlier question. "He just needs some exercising."

Already, the horse's gait was easier as he walked alongside Mareen around the pen.

"Do you think it'll come to injections?" Mareen asked.

Brig said nothing. It took the silence stretching on for longer than a few seconds for Brig to realize that the question was aimed at her. She was so used to one of her other sisters shouting out the answer that it took her an additional moment to respond to Mareen's question.

"No, I don't think you need to go the pharmaceutical route if you don't want to. We can do supplements to start. Right now, I think he needs routine, exercise, and a modified diet. If we can get some of this weight off, he'll feel an immediate difference."

"Thank you, Brig," said Mareen. "For taking care of him all these years."

Brig shrugged. "You would've done the same for me."

Mareen looked pensive. For so many years, Mareen had tried to hide her true feelings. Over the past week that she'd been with her family on the ranch, that skill was getting harder and harder to maintain.

Mareen wasn't used to others having her back. Even her own mother had used her as a pawn in the divorce. That divide had left Mareen feeling alone, even though she had a big family who had always wanted to love her. Now, Mareen just needed to learn to let them.

Brig insinuated herself between Mareen and the horse. It was easy for Mareen to show her love for the horse. It wasn't so easy to show it to her sisters. At least not yet.

"Resistance is futile," said Brig as she leaned into her older sister. "I don't doubt it for a second you would do whatever it takes to keep us all safe. You nearly married a man you didn't love to keep a roof over our head."

Mareen relaxed into Brig's embrace. She was doing that faster and faster these days, after always holding herself off from her sisters. Brig had always ignored that barrier Mareen had tried to erect. She didn't believe in the term half-sisters. All five of her siblings were all hers regardless of the imaginary lines their parents and others may have drawn in the dirt.

"I didn't do the best job of saving you," said Mareen. "You still have to marry a stranger."

"Carter isn't a stranger," piped in Tilly. Her face hunkered down in her phone as usual. "Did you know he worked for Dad since he joined the military? It means he's practically our brother."

Mareen and Brig shared a glance. Tilly didn't catch it. She was often oblivious until the thing was staring her right in the face.

"I didn't know that about him," Brig said, deciding to skirt the brother comment.

"Yeah, didn't he tell you?" said Tilly, her thumbs tapping away on her phone's face.

"Carter and I have never had an actual conversation."

"Sure you have," said Tilly. "We were all talking last night."

"The two of you were talking. I was simply in your presence."

Tilly's thumbs paused, hovering over her phone. Finally, she glanced up. "What do you mean by that?"

"Do you realize Carter is the longest relationship you've ever had?" said Brig.

"Relationship?" Tilly frowned, her thumbs caressing the side of her phone case. "Carter and I are just friends."

Brig turned back to Mareen. She felt gratified when Mareen lifted an eyebrow, indicating that she was seeing exactly what Brig was seeing. Tilly was entirely clueless.

"Carter's for you," Tilly said.

"Thanks, sis," Brig scoffed. "Are you giving him to me with a big red bow?"

Tilly frowned, completely missing the jab. "You're being a child."

It was the insult often hurled at Brig when her older sisters didn't have an adequate comeback. Only this time, it wasn't going to work. Brig was tired of pretending, tired of playing this childish game of peekaboo where she was the wizard behind the curtain.

"Why does everyone accuse me of that when I tell a truth they don't like?" she said.

Tilly looked to Mareen for support. Mareen wisely kept to the other side of the pen, making sure to avoid any new lines drawn in this family.

"I'm going on a date with Sergei this weekend." Tilly held up her phone. "Which proves I'm not into Carter. And he's not into me. He's helping me plan my outfit."

Mareen crossed the imaginary line. She and Colonel Brandon stood firmly on Brig's side. It was a moot point as Tilly was back looking down at her phone.

Brig's attention wasn't on her sister any longer. Jackson was walking toward them. For the first time since he'd arrived on the ranch, his gaze wasn't on anyone and anything besides her. Jackson was looking at and walking toward Brig with even, purposeful strides.

CHAPTER THIRTEEN

Jackson's gaze slid over Brig as he walked toward her and her sisters. For the past few weeks, he'd been sure to look past her. Not today. Today, something had changed.

She wore a pair of jeans he'd seen on her many times before. The fabric molded to curves he'd never admit to noticing. The dull colors of her flannel shirt only served to brighten the mischievous glint in her blue eyes. Her toned arms moved as she expertly and confidently handled the horse in her care.

Even on the days when he'd tried not to look, Jackson had always noticed that Brig knew exactly what she was doing when it came to the horses under her care. The horses knew too, and they followed her commands without dallying. With a wave of her hand, one of the horses came to her.

Jackson felt his feet pick up their pace as he rushed to fulfill the order. The walk down the path did him good in more ways than one. His knee was feeling nearly brand new. And so was his mind, thanks to the talk with Father Matthews.

It was as though shells had fallen from his eyes. Brig stood backlit by the sun. In the glare of the afternoon light, Jackson saw the young woman in an entirely new way.

As though she felt his gaze, Brig looked up from the horse, and her eyes found Jackson's. Jackson nearly stumbled when they did.

Gone from her eyes was playfulness. Instead, her gaze was cool, medical assessment as it zeroed in on his right. Her head cocked to one side and then the other as though she was measuring each of his strides.

Jackson's back went erect. He felt every muscle in his legs working to win her approval. He almost wished for the days when she'd grin at him like a lovesick schoolgirl. When her gaze lifted to his face and met his, there was no hint of that girl. In fact, Jackson couldn't remember how he'd ever seen

Brigadear Silver as a kid with all the weight of intelligence in those blue eyes.

"You're being a child."

Jackson frowned at Tilly's accusation. It didn't fit the woman standing before him. Brig stood with a strong posture. Her head high. Her brow quirked.

"Why does everyone accuse me of that when I tell a truth they don't like?"

That stopped Jackson in his tracks. He'd done the same to her the other day. He'd heard her sisters do it more than once since he'd been on the ranch.

Each time the childish accusation was hurled at her, Brig would shrug it off. She didn't now. Jackson wasn't sure what the sisters were arguing about. He could see that it was Tilly who looked like a petulant adolescent. It was Brig who looked on with the wary patience of an overworked mother.

That cracked a smile on his lips. His smile quickly fell when he saw that Brig wasn't smiling. She looked defeated.

"Fine," Brig said when they were upon them. "Have it your way."

Brig came toward them. But her gaze wasn't on Jackson. Her attention focused in on Carter. "How are you this morning, Carter?"

Carter startled. His body had been angled to

keep walking past Brig. He was likely headed for the object of his unspoken desire; Tilly. But he stopped and gave Brig a bright smile.

"I'm doing good." He paused a beat. And then, "And you?"

"I'm doing great," said Brig.

A silence descended between the two. Had it been a couple of days ago, Jackson would've nudged Carter to ask after Brig's health or to give her a compliment. Today Jackson was annoyed that Brig's attention was on his friend and not him.

"I think it's time we got to know each other," said Brig. "Since we're going to be married soon."

In that moment, Jackson knew bliss. He stood in a state of perfect happiness and joy. He was oblivious to everything around him. All he could see was his future with Brig.

Caramel-skinned cherubs with light blue eyes and wild curly hair running around his legs. His hands clasped with Brig's as he looked down into her beautiful face. Her lips pressed against his in one of a million kisses he'd steal because it was his right as her-

The record scratch of his dream made Jackson wince. Brig's words hadn't been aimed at him. They'd been for Carter.

Beside Jackson, Carter blinked. "Right. Sure. Of course."

Wrong. Doubtful. Never going to happen. That's what Jackson wanted to shout.

"Why don't we go for a walk," Carter said as he took a step toward Brig.

At least Carter had tried to take a step toward Brig. But something held him back. Jackson looked over to see that it was his arm against his friend's chest.

"No," Jackson barked. The bass in his voice was so deep that the horse took a step back. "I need to talk to Brig first. About my knee. She's my doctor."

"She's not a doctor," Tilly muttered.

"Brig?" Jackson held his hand out to her.

Brig stared at his open palm as though he was presenting her with a sparkly diamond. He didn't miss the grin as she slid her hand into his. Jackson fought to keep his hold on her light.

He failed. His fingers clasped firmly around hers, not letting in a whisper of air between them. Silence reigned behind them as they walked off toward the barn.

Great. Now that Jackson had her, he wasn't sure what to do with her. He just knew that her hand in his felt right, and he didn't want to let her go. The real question was, was he going to keep her?

The second the thought crossed his mind, Jackson realized his miscalculation. He was alone. In a barn. With Brig. A position he'd promised himself he'd never get in.

Yet here he was. A man unarmed against his most worthy adversary. The war was already decided, had been when the general had ordered them all to come here. But Jackson wasn't going down the aisle without a fight. If he didn't at least show some gumption, he wouldn't be the man deserving of the general's daughter.

ingles shot up and zinged down Brig's entire arm at just the touch of Jackson's warm hand on hers. When the door to the barn closed behind him, she heard his sharp intake of breath.

At first, she was concerned that it was pain. But he was moving with sure strides beside her. That wasn't physical pain he was feeling. It was something deeper. It was the sound he'd made a week ago when they'd all been playing Monopoly, and she'd bankrupted him even though he owned all the expensive, blue properties.

Jackson hadn't realized he'd been had. Right up until she had him. Once again, Brig had snuck up on him and was ready to take him for everything he had. Only this time, in return, she'd offer him her heart.

She stopped and turned to face him. Jackson was looking at her, but she wasn't sure what he was seeing. His features were a mask. She knew he had to be feeling this too. How much longer would he deny what was happening between them?

"So," Brig began once they were standing in the barn. "You got me alone. Now, what are you going to do with me?"

Jackson said nothing as his gaze appraised her. Brig noted he still held her hand in his. She'd always hated when her sisters held her hand. She knew they liked babying her, but by the time she was a teenager it had gotten old.

Of course, it felt different when a man held her hand; when this man held her hand. So, Brig didn't pull away from Jackson's hold. She wanted to be held by him.

He'd called her baby when they'd been trapped in the exam room back in the clinic. Brig had always cringed when guys tried that endearment on her. When Jackson had said it in that deep voice of his, it sounded as though she was something precious, someone he wanted to care for. Maybe even cradle in his arms.

Jackson dropped her hand. He re-schooled his features. Now he looked at her with clinical assessment.

"I want to talk with you about my care plan," he said.

"Your… care plan?"

He nodded. "I think you were right about my treatment."

"You… do?"

"I'd like to get started on your suggestions."

"Oh. Okay."

"I was thinking we could take a walk. Maybe a long one. Down by the pond between the Flying Cross and Silver Star property line. Since that's a long walk, maybe we should take a picnic lunch."

"Hang on." Brig held up her hands, needing a minute to follow Jackson's new plan. She opened her mouth to take a deep breath. The air she had been holding inside gushed out first. She had to take another moment for her lungs to refill before she could speak. "You want to take a long walk with me and have a picnic?"

Jackson nodded patiently. His features still set in that unreadable expression. "Yes, if that sounds like a good care plan to you."

"It sounds like a date to me."

His features barely shifted. Brig caught the slight wince of his right eye. Or was that a wink? She'd become very familiar with Jackson's looks of pain. There was none in the crinkle of his eye. So she decided to label that a wink.

The next thing she noted was a slight tug of his bottom lip. He wasn't frowning. Frowns were signs of distaste. People didn't lick their lip when something was distasteful. They licked their lip when they wanted to taste something.

Meaning Jackson wanted to taste her. Brig wanted to jump up and down and pump her fists for joy. But she couldn't. The game wasn't won. Yet. She was going to make this grown man cry uncle.

"I'll have to ask Carter since, you know, I'm engaged to him."

Jackson lips pressed into a flat line as though he'd tasted a rotten egg. "You are not marrying Carter."

"I'm afraid I'll have to." Brig raised her open palms in a helpless gesture. "Unless there's an alternative."

Jackson's body was so tense, so rigid, that Brig worried he might hurt himself. She would be the one to cry uncle if she sensed that he was in pain. She reached out her hand and laid it on his chest. His heart was racing.

"Are you okay?" she asked.

Jackson let out a long, weary sigh as though the weight of the world had just left his strong shoulders. "When you touch me, all the pain goes away. You make me feel like I can do anything."

His hand covered hers. It pressed her palm flat against his chest, where his heart lay. Brig wanted to curl her fingers into him. She wanted to possess this man completely, as he had possessed her the first time she'd laid eyes on him.

"You can do anything," she said. "And if you let me, I'll stand beside you as your helpmate, as your cheerleader, as your partner while you do. Every day, for the rest of my life."

Jackson's hazel gaze roamed every inch of her face. As he did so, he came closer, closer. Then his free hand shot out.

He wasn't cradling her. He was holding her so tight she couldn't tell where she ended, and he began. She didn't feel like a baby in his arms. She felt perfect. Right.

And then his lips met hers.

She'd expected Jackson to crash into her with how tightly he was holding her. Instead, his lips were the gentlest of caresses. A helpless moan escaped her lips. She'd spent all these weeks trying to bend Jackson to her will that she was surprised at her cry of surrender.

Brig had fought for his attention. She had fought for him to see her as a woman. Now the battle was won, and she was lost.

Jackson's hold on her tightened even more as he deepened the kiss. In this realm, she was out of her depths. She'd received a few light pecks, but she'd never opened to someone as she was doing now. Jackson invaded, and Brig let down all of her defenses. She laid her every weapon at his feet.

Until he was wrenched from her.

Brig opened her eyes to see a haze of brown hair and a fist flying. She tensed for impact. But the punch landed on Jackson's nose. He went down like a stone.

"Scout!" Brig shouted, grabbing at her sister's hooked right arm, which was preparing to unload again. "Stop it!"

CHAPTER FIFTEEN

One moment, Jackson was tasting heaven. Brig was sweeter than he'd imagined. With the first brush of her upper lip, the sugar rush had weakened his knees. His second nip of her lower lip sent energy beaming out from his chest and down into his legs.

He felt like he could run a marathon. He felt like he could climb a mountain. He felt invincible with this bountiful, beautiful, blooming slice of pure bliss.

Jackson pulled her closer to deepen the kiss. But instead of more bliss, he tasted blood.

"Get your hands off my sister."

The sharp pain in his face was intense after the tender feel of Brig's lips. He'd already lost his breath while kissing her. Now he needed air. His throbbing nose wouldn't let any in. Likely due to the blood filling his nostrils. The pendulum of sensations was so violent that Jackson could no longer hold himself up.

He went down. Luckily, it was his left knee that crashed into the dirt floor of the barn and not his right. It still hurt, adding to the agony of his busted nose.

"I don't know what game you're playing, but I'm ending it now."

Even with his eyes closed and his nose aching, Jackson knew that voice. It had lost its femininity and sounded much more like the general who had given him orders for years. When he opened his eyes, Scout Silver Rawlings loomed over him like an avenging angel of death.

It should've smarted that a woman had gotten the drop on him. But Brig had already brought Jackson to his knees the moment he set foot on this ranch. It had been inevitable that he would fall for the girl. So, taking a blow from her older, over-protective sister -who by the way had a mean right hook- was his due.

"She's just a kid," Scout snarled.

"She's not a kid," Jackson said at the same time that Brig said, "I'm not a kid."

Brig's arms were around him. He'd like to say that the moment she touched him, all the pain went away. If only that were true. It wasn't.

The pain did dull as Brig cradled his head in her hands. She tilted his head from side to side and then back. Jackson clamped his mouth shut from the vertigo. Then he howled in pain when she touched his injured nose.

"Ouch, Brig!"

"It's not broken."

Maybe not, but her fingers pressing into either side of his nostrils wasn't helping any. If they survived this, they needed to have a serious talk about her bedside manner when it came to treating human patients.

"You're supposed to be marrying Gunny," said Scout.

"I'm not marrying Gunny," Jackson said at the same time that Brig said, "He's not marrying Gunny."

"He's marrying me," Brig said at the same time that Jackson said, "I'm marrying Brig."

In the barn door, a crowd gathered. Linc stood just inside the barn, his arms crossed over his shoulder as he grinned at his wife's back while simultaneously wincing down at Jackson.

Tilly and Carter stood off to the side of the

entrance. For once, they weren't looking down at a cell phone and cracking jokes. But like always, their heads were together as they watched the spectacle with voyeuristic delight.

In front of Jackson, Scout's right fist was still cocked. Jackson had been trying to get his feet under him. One glance at the weapon of Scout's hand, and he sat his bum down on the ground in surrender. Linc gave him a nod as though he'd made the right decision.

General Silver had taught them many lessons in combat over the years. They knew the signals of when to advance on a fledgling enemy. They knew when to press the bad guys into making a mistake that would give them a tactical advantage. They'd also learned when the odds were against them and to throw up the white flag.

Jackson's white shirt was now dripping with red. His fledgling defenses which Brig had masterfully broken down, lay in shambles. As one sister stood over him with fists at the ready, and the other continued to poke at his nose in a sign of care, he decided to let the two superior forces duke it out amongst themselves.

"You broke his nose, Scouttie."

"I'm about to do more than that," Scout huffed.

"He seduced you."

Brig snorted as she glared up at her sister. "I seduced him."

Jackson winced. Not at the pain, but because Brig was right. She had put him completely under his spell, and he was quite content to stay there for the rest of his days.

"He's too old for you," Scout insisted.

"He's eight years older than me," said Brig.

"I'm actually nine years older," Jackson said. "Closer to ten. I'll be thirty this year."

"You're not helping," Brig hissed.

"It's the same age difference as your parents," Jackson said to Scout, who had taken a step closer to them.

"Again," said Brig, "you're not helping."

"I don't believe in divorce." Jackson turned his gaze from Scout and focused all of his attention on Brig. "So, if you say yes, it's for better or—"

"Yes." Brig grinned, tears lighting her eyes.

Despite the pain still lingering in his body, Jackson reached up to cup Brig's chin. It trembled at his touch. "I haven't asked the question yet."

"When you do, the answer will be yes."

Brig moved closer, tilting her head first one way then the other. Her nose still bumped his before he could taste her lips. Jackson pulled back with a pained groan. Less from the pain and more from being denied the sweet taste of the woman who would soon be his wife.

"I haven't said yes," said Scout.

"It's not your decision, Scouttie," said Brig.

"What about Carter?" said Scout.

"She'd run over Carter," said Jackson.

"Hey!" Carter said from the door of the barn.

"They're right," Tilly said to him.

That appeared to soothe Carter. He shrugged and offered Jackson a grin that said congratulations, and I pity you at the same time.

"You think she won't run over you?" said Scout to Jackson.

Jackson looked back at Brig. She was beaming at him. Her cheeks glowed in the low light of the barn. The happiness in her smile soothed every ache in his knee, every pain in his nose.

"I'm sure she will. But I can handle her."

That glow of happiness morphed into the mischievous grin that Jackson had once feared. Only now, he realized it hadn't been fear of danger or a threat. Jackson was a warrior, and the fight-or-flight part of him had known that that grin would be his downfall.

Not a fall to defeat.

The type of fall that involved his heart.

Jackson was going to fall in love with Brigadear Silver. He might already be there. He was down on the ground after all. And that grin on her face seemed to say this was exactly how she'd planned all of this to go down.

He was so screwed. And he didn't mind one bit. He pulled her to him and pressed a light kiss to her lips. Their noses tweaked, and he winced in pain, but it was a good hurt.

CHAPTER SIXTEEN

"Aren't we walking?"

In answer to Jackson's question, Brig led him inside the barn where two horses were saddled. She would never tire of the deep rumble of Jackson's voice. Nor how it rolled through her body when he spoke. She wouldn't have to worry about never getting enough of him because she finally had him. Which meant that she wouldn't have to hide her feelings for him any longer.

Jackson was hers. He'd made a promise, which for a man of his honor made it a done deal. But soon, she'd have it made official in a legally binding contract, which she'd never let him get out of.

Luckily, it looked like he was pretty happy with his acquisition. His fingers twined with hers. Just at the knuckles, not down to the webbing between each digit. It was more than enough for her.

Brig reveled in the feel of his callused hands against hers. She shivered every time his bare forearm brushed against hers. If just the touch of his elbow made her warm, imagine what another kiss would do.

Then she realized she could have his lips pressed against hers anytime she wanted. Because Jackson was hers. He was going to marry her. They would spend the rest of their days with him whispering in her ear, brushing light kisses on her mouth, and doing all the things married couples did to cause shivers.

"Brig?"

"No, we're not walking." Brig reluctantly pulled off her fiancée hat and pulled on her clinical one. "You've had enough weight on your knee for now."

"I'm not sure if you're calling me fat? Or if you're judging my stamina."

Brig giggled. Then she rested her hand on Jackson's chest. Just because she now had that right as his fiancée. Jackson didn't shy away from her touch.

"No one could get away with calling you out of shape," she said.

Jackson huffed, a dark shadow crossing his

features. Part of Brig wanted to poke at that, to unfurl his brow and ask more about the shadow. She decided to focus on the second part of his statement.

"As for your stamina…"

Jackson quirked a brow at her.

"We'll have to see about that."

Brig tilted her head up, angling for a kiss.

Jackson's lips parted. Then he gulped audibly. As though he was swallowing down his desire.

Brig didn't move an inch. She didn't bat an eyelash. She held her position and waited. Her fiancé needed to figure out that the only thing standing between them was him.

"We're waiting until we're married," Jackson said, his lips hovering just above hers. Because his mouth was so close to hers, she felt his lips quiver as he said the words, as though the thoughts that made them up stood on shaky ground.

"Get your mind out of the gutter, soldier," Brig said against his lips. Then she leaned her head back so that he could see the seriousness in her gaze. "We're going horseback riding. A little equine therapy will be good for that injury."

Jackson let out the breath he'd been holding. That gush of air didn't sound relieved. It was sweet with his desire for her.

"I'm going to be a good wife to you; hopefully, a great wife. But I'm outstanding at what I do in rehabilitative care. I'll get your knee where you want it to be."

Jackson brushed a finger across her temple. His knee brushed against hers as they stood toe to toe. "My knee is exactly where I want it to be."

His lips brushed hers in a slow caress. By the time he'd brushed from one side of her mouth to the other, Brig had forgotten where they were, why they were there, and what her name was. Before she could press him to deepen the kiss, Jackson hoisted her up and onto one of the horses.

"Hey," she protested. "No more heavy lifting, mister."

"You're light as a feather," Jackson said as he mounted his horse.

He gave her a wink before urging his horse on. Brig let him take the lead. He was a man, and they needed to feel in control from time to time.

"Sit up taller," Brig said once they were on the trails.

Jackson glanced over at her. The man swaggered in the saddle as though he were walking across the runway. It took Brig a moment before she could remember what she'd said and why.

"I'm the expert, remember."

Jackson gave her a sultry smile and did as she bade. With his shoulders back, he looked even more devastating in the saddle.

"Riding is a three-dimensional movement," Brig went on, trying to focus on his health and not how beautifully masculine he was. "Your body is moving back and forward, up and down, and side to side all at once when you're riding a horse. It's the same as when you're walking. You're using all the same neuromuscular pathways as when your arms swing back and forward, your hips move side to side, and your legs go up and down. Except now, you're not using your body weight."

Jackson adjusted his body in the saddle as he listened. Then he grinned as he looked at her. "You're good."

"No," she corrected. "I'm exceptional."

"Lean to the side," he said.

Brig grinned as she did so. The horses came to walk side by side. Jackson leaned toward her from his mount. He brushed a gentle kiss against her lips. Brig wanted more but now was not the time.

Still, when they pulled apart, a mischievous grin lit her face. "Ready to kick it up a notch?"

"Bring it on."

Brig urged her horse up from a walk and into a slightly faster trot. Jackson did the same, still keeping his same posture. Brig watched for a moment, checking his body's alignment. When she was satisfied, she went faster. Jackson matched her pace for pace, his posture never wavering.

By the time they came to a stop, all four of them —man, woman, and horses—were out of breath. Jackson and Brig tied the horses up in a patch of grass with flowers they liked. With their rides settled, they made their picnic.

Jackson spread the blanket while Brig unpacked the food. Once the feast was spread, Jackson picked up a piece of fruit and brought it to Brig's mouth.

"Are you going to feed me like a child?" she asked. "Because if we're still on this age thing, I think I'll be the one cutting up your food in fifty years, Boomer."

"No, baby," he grinned.

The way Jackson said baby made Brig feel nothing like a young girl. That word rumbled in his mouth, making her feel like a desirable woman.

"I stopped seeing a child back at the clinic. Probably sooner than that, which is why I've been trying to avoid you the past couple of weeks. Right now, I'm feeding you this food because I want any excuse to touch your lips."

"You don't need any excuse. I'm yours."

Jackson ran the chunk of fruit over Brig's bottom lip. She opened and took a bite. The fruit's juices ran down her chin. Jackson caught the droplets with his thumb. Then he put his thumb in his mouth.

"Not as sweet as you," he said.

Brig expected that to be followed up by more kisses where they completely ignored all the food and feasted on each other. Instead, Jackson's gaze clouded over and threatened to rain on their picnic.

"You have your whole life ahead of you," he said. "Am I being selfish taking it away?"

"I want to experience my life with you at my side. I want to be by your side. You're going to need a nursemaid in your old age, boomer."

Jackson chuckled. "Hopefully, by then, you'll have learned better bedside manners, baby."

"I love you, Jackson."

She couldn't help the words. They tumbled out with a will of their own because they were the truth. Thankfully, Jackson didn't flinch at the declaration.

"Don't tell me it's too soon. Or that I don't know you well enough. I know my own mind, and I know what's in my heart."

Her sisters tried to tell her what was best for her all her life. But she knew no one would be better for her than this man. Jackson had seen right through to the heart of her since that first day. No one had bothered to look that deeply. Finally, he wasn't running from what he saw. He reached for her.

"I'm going to spend my life being worthy of your love, Brigadear. Even with these rickety, old man bones."

"Okay, boomer," she grinned.

"Come here, baby." Jackson captured her lips in that grin.

Their picnic lunch did sit forgotten on the blanket. By the time the sun began to set, both Jackson and Brig were full from feasting on each other's lips.

CHAPTER SEVENTEEN

She loved him.

The thought should send Jackson running for the hills. It should have him turning her around and pushing her back to her sisters. Instead, Jackson held Brig's hand as though it were his lifeline.

Because that's what she was. Just the touch of her hand was more potent than the pills he'd taken every morning since the blast. This morning he hadn't reached for the cursed bottle. He hadn't felt the need. After the workout from yesterday, coupled with the warmth that had suffused his limbs from holding her close and kissing her soundly, the constant aches and pains of his body had retreated.

Brig's fingers twined with his over the middle

console of the truck. She hummed along to the radio in the passenger seat of the car. Her gaze was out the window. Her features were relaxed, as though she didn't have a care in the world.

Why would she have a care? She had gotten everything she wanted. One of those things was him. Because make no mistake, Jackson Bennett was wrapped around Brigadear Silver's little finger, and he wasn't making a move to unravel himself from his position.

Had he have known that being with her would put such a kick in his step and lift his spirits, he would've let her trap him the first day he'd set foot on the ranch. Right now, he brought her fingers to his lips and brushed kisses from her knuckles to her nails. Brig turned from her sightseeing out the window. When those blue eyes landed on him, Jackson knew peace for the first time in his life.

He'd thought her mischievous grin would be the death of him. He'd come to see her in a new light when wisdom brightened her gaze. Now, only love and devotion shined through.

He pulled the truck into the first parking spot he found. Then he divulged them both of their seatbelts and pulled her to him. Brig wrapped her arms around his neck with a delighted giggle.

Jackson kissed her like it was their first time. Like it was their last time. Like they had all the time in the world.

But they didn't. Brig nudged at his shoulder as she tried to pull away from him. Jackson growled and held her tighter.

"Jackson, I have to get to class."

"Of course, I'd wind up with the nerdy teacher's pet," Jackson sighed but loosened his grip.

She gave him a wink as she slung her backpack over her shoulder. "You don't have to wait. This will take a few hours."

"I'm not leaving you here stranded."

"I don't want to ruin your day. I can get a friend to drive me back or call an Uber."

Jackson cupped her chin in his hand, tilting her head back so that she would see the dead seriousness in his gaze. "First, you could never ruin my day. Second, I'm going to be your husband. That means it will be your job to inconvenience me."

Desire and delight churned in Brig's blue gaze. Jackson couldn't help himself. He leaned over the middle console to taste the emotions on her face, starting with her eyelids, then her cheekbones, and finally her lips. She was even sweeter than the last time he'd kissed her. Now that he was allowed, he couldn't seem to stop kissing Brig.

"I'll wait for you," he said when he pulled away.

"Okay," she agreed.

Jackson blinked once, twice, and then held his gaze wide. "So that's how it's done? That's how I get you to do what you're told?"

Brig leaned in, just a few millimeters from his lips. "Kiss me like that, and I'll obey your every command."

"Dutifully noted."

Jackson snuck a quick kiss, savoring the taste of her grin. Then he slipped out of his seatbelt and opened the driver's side door to round to her side. When he stepped down, he misjudged the distance to the paved street.

Pain shot up his knee. So swift, so absolute, that he felt nauseous. He made a sound at the back of his throat like a pained animal. A few people stopped walking to glance over.

"You okay?" Brig had hopped out and was beside him.

"I'm good." Jackson didn't look at her as he straightened. His gaze was on the eyes staring at him. Young eyes taking him in. Pity on their faces.

"We may have overworked it on the ride yesterday," Brig said. "Will you promise to take it easy while I'm inside?"

Jackson wasn't listening. He was glaring at the young men eyeing Brig's backside. She was still bent down, running her hands over his knee. Jackson pulled her up and into his arms in a possessive grip.

That gesture broke the young men's lurid stares. They looked from him to Brig and back again at him. Then they sniggered as they walked on.

Jackson wanted to storm over to them and teach them the real lesson they should be learning on this campus. But his knee ached. He'd probably wobble as he marched over.

"Why don't you catch a movie at the town cinema," said Brig, completely oblivious to the battle lines drawn behind her. "They have a matinee."

"Senior citizens go to the matinees."

"Then you'll be right at home, boomer."

Part of his brain knew that the nickname was a joke, a private joke shared between the two of them. But Jackson was still raw from the pain in his knee and the adrenaline pumping through his veins at the threats now jogging away from them to join a game of Ultimate Frisbee.

"I think I'll hit the gym," Jackson said.

"No, you won't." Brig's voice was loud enough to carry.

Jackson drew up to his full height, towering over her. Of course, that wouldn't deter Brig. She threw her head back and glared right back at him.

"I'm the boss of your body," she said, placing her hand on his heart. "You're the boss of my heart. If you break your body, it will break my heart."

This little slip of a woman. How did she unman him and at the same time make him feel invincible? Jackson knew there was no choice but to do as she told him.

She leaned in for a kiss. Once again, Jackson obeyed. Just because he could, he deepened the kiss, pressing her to him and giving anyone who walked by a show. Those frat boys were off catching a frisbee, but they wouldn't get their hands on this ultimate prize.

After a few catcalls, Jackson was satisfied that he had made his point. When he let her go, it was Brig who stumbled a few steps as she made her way to her classroom.

"To the happy couple," said Carter, raising his glass.

Everyone around the table did the same. The entire Silver clan took up a long table in the back of the bar. Even though they were in the private area, there still weren't enough seats for all eleven of them. The three married couples didn't mind. As always, Scout and Linc, Saylor and Jeff, and Mareen and Wilson used one seat per couple.

Brig sat beside Jackson, but their chairs were so close together that she was nearly on his lap.

"And here's to you, Jackson," Carter turned to face his friend. "Only man I don't mind losing my fiancée to."

Jackson tipped back his beer as he drank to his

friend's toast. His arm rested lightly around Brig's shoulders, but his fingers gripped her shoulder cap in what felt like mindless possession. Brig didn't mind at all.

"Thank you for being so good about it," said Brig, raising her Shirley Temple to Carter. The fizzy drink tickled her nose when she brought the glass to her mouth. The sugar rush made her blink a couple of times.

"You chose the better man, Brig." Carter bent down and bussed her on the cheek.

Jackson growled, giving his friend a look of warning. That low hum only served to increase the bubble of sweet happiness that Brig found herself in. Carter held up his hands in protest and backed away.

"So..." said Tilly. "What are we going to tell Gunny?"

All around the table, drinks paused on their way to mouths. Those who had taken a drink gulped down the contents. No one spoke.

"We'll tell her that she got an upgrade," Carter said, brushing imaginary dust off his shoulders.

"You'll marry her instead?" asked Tilly. She placed the phone she always held face down on the table.

"Of course," Carter said, turning to her. "It's what I agreed to."

Tilly nodded. She didn't pick her phone back up. She tapped her nails on the back of the case.

"Now you just have to land Sergei," said Carter.

"Sergei's out," said Tilly, picking her phone back up. "Can you believe he DM'd me at one in the morning with a *U up?*"

"Rookie move," said Carter.

"Right?" agreed Tilly.

"But you were up," said Mareen. "You and Carter were watching *Say Anything.* Again."

"We could hear Peter Gabriel singing *In Your Eyes* blaring like he was holding a stereo right into our window."

Mareen shuddered. Wilson pulled her into his chest, pressing his lips against her temple. The newlyweds had the unfortunate luck to be in the cabin nearest Carter's, which Tilly had built. Tilly stayed in a bedroom in the main house most nights, but she could often be found hanging out in her old cabin with Carter.

"I thought you two hated the eighties," Wilson said.

"We do," said Tilly.

"Then why are you always watching John Hughes films?" asked Mareen.

"Making fun," said Carter.

"It's called hate-watching," said Tilly.

Brig lost interest in the nonsensical conversation. Tilly had a habit of only watching movies and television shows she swore she detested. She'd talk all through them, commenting on how stupid a character was or how tragic their outfit was. No surprise that none of her sisters enjoyed going out to the movies with her. But Carter seemed to enjoy her every quip.

Brig turned from her family's back and forth to the dance floor. Her toes tapped in time to the beat. She'd been sitting at a desk all day filling out charts and reports as part of her classwork at the clinic. Now she wanted to move her body. But she didn't get out of her seat because she also was happy right where she was.

Jackson had an arm around her shoulder. She was pressed flush against his side. Every now and again, he'd lean over and brush his lips against her cheekbone in a thoughtless kiss, as though he'd been doing it all her life. Why would she pass up this spot? It was the best seat in the bar.

Party in the USA came on the speakers. Brig

couldn't resist. When Miley sang about putting her hands up, Brig threw up her hands and shimmied her shoulders.

"Go dance, Hannah," said Tilly.

"Hannah?" asked Jackson.

"Hannah Montana. It was her favorite show as a kid."

"Oh, right. You told me." Jackson grinned at her. "You wanna dance, baby?"

"Do you wanna dance with me, boomer?"

"Ha ha," snorted Carter. "Baby boomer. Get it."

"Yeah, I get it," said Tilly.

Jackson ignored them both. His lips twisted as though he wasn't happy with the words he was about to say. "I don't dance."

"Oh." Brig felt her shoulders hunch. "Okay."

"The knee," Jackson clarified. "Doctor's orders."

"Well, your doctor thinks you can sway from side to side while you have her in your arms."

Slowly, Jackson's lips untwisted from their grimace and turned into a grin. "That sounds like the best medication ever."

He got up, holding out his hand to her. Brig slipped her hand in his, feeling a jolt of excitement go through her. It wasn't their first dance as a married couple. That was coming soon. It was their first dance as a couple which was more important. Not everyone would be invited to her wedding. But when the bar-goers saw them in a tight clench, everyone would know that Jackson was her man and she was his woman.

Jackson led her to the dance floor. Once in the center of the gyrating bodies, he gave her a slow twirl. Once she came back around to face him, Brig rested her hands on his shoulders. She moved her hips, but not in time to the beat. She moved in time to the beating of Jackson's heart. Jackson kept a light hand on her as she moved around.

"Your beautiful," he said in her ear when he pulled her close. "I'm the luckiest man in the world."

Brig wrapped her arms around his neck, swaying slowly to the fast-paced beat. Even though her feet were steady and Jackson's hold was firm, Brig felt like she was falling.

"When I hold you close, I feel invincible. Like I can run a marathon. Or even bust a dance move."

And then he did. He pulled away from her, crossed one foot over the other, and did a spin that would've put James Brown to shame.

"Where'd you get those moves?" called a guy. "Send them back to the seventies."

The carefree joy on Jackson's face melted away.

His head snapped to the side to find the taunting voice. Brig looked over and recognized a couple of guys from campus. She'd never had any classes with them. They seemed to spend their days on the lawn playing Ultimate Frisbee and catcalling at the girls walking by. A few of the young women on campus had filed a complaint, but not much had been done.

Jackson tensed as though he was ready to do something. Brig wrapped her arm around his bicep. She didn't want her night ruined.

She should've known Jackson wouldn't fall for such childish behavior. He gave the boys a warning glare. Then he swayed with Brig until they were away from the menace.

Brig grinned up at him. Some of the tension left his face as he gazed down at her. A second later, his back was ramrod straight, as though he was tensed to fight.

"Come on, sweet thing," said the same nasally voice. "You know you wanna hang with us instead of the old geezer here."

Though the kid might be on the college campus, he couldn't have been enrolled there. No one was that dumb. He'd riled up a trained soldier. Even worse, he was on the bad side of a Silver sister's temper.

As though they sensed danger, her sisters were already rising from their seats at the back of the bar. But by the time Brig turned back around, Jackson already had the guy in hand.

Literally. With one hand, he had the boy's shirt collar gathered in his fist. The boy struggled to breathe as Jackson lifted him an inch off the ground.

The kid was helpless. Or so she thought. Mr. Mouthy's hands slapped ineffectually at Jackson's iron grip. But when his sneakered shoe kicked out, that was all it took.

The toe of Mouthy's shoe struck Jackson right in the wrong knee cap. Jackson's grip opened, and both men went down.

CHAPTER NINETEEN

"Surgery."

There were words before that pronouncement. There were words after it. But all Jackson heard was that single word.

Surgery.

Nearly two hours ago, his friends had hefted him off the dance floor. They'd laid him out in the backseat of one of the cars and took off to the Emergency Room. Brig had climbed into the backseat with him. Jackson's head had rested in her lap. He'd tried to concentrate on the feel of her fingers in his hair, on his cheek, on his chest. Instead, he felt every rock and pebble the wheels bumped over on the way to the hospital. Luckily, with it being a small town, they didn't have to go far.

Jackson had refused any pain meds when they'd wheeled him in. He'd been off Fentanyl for a few days now with no adverse reactions. He didn't want to backstep. Though he knew that the time of grinning and bearing it would be cut short all too soon. All he felt were the sharp pains going up and down his leg, radiating outward from the throb in his kneecap.

There was one bright spot of relief in all of the pain. Brig. She stood at the bed beside him. Her gaze fixed on the doctor as the young man spoke.

The youthful doctor looked like he was just out of high school with his pimpled face and slim build. Was that a lisp Jackson detected as the boy said words like arthroplasty and synovial membrane? Was Jackson really going to listen to his prognosis?

No, he wasn't. He was getting up and walking out of here before this boy picked a knife and started playing with it near Jackson's knee. But even shifting on the bed caused shooting pains to run up and down his leg.

Jackson slumped back on the hospital bed. Brig leaned over him, peering into his gaze and running her hand over his leg at the same time. Her fingers were careful not to touch his knee.

A part of Jackson knew that her touch would be just the thing to heal him. Instead, the young doctor touched him. Jackson let out a howl of pain that nearly knocked him out.

Brig's blue gaze widened. There wasn't mischief in her eyes. Nor was their wisdom. Her bright blue depths dimmed to showcase dismay and dread.

"I'm not having surgery," Jackson managed to bite out. "The swelling will go down, like before. I'll just stay off it for a few days."

Brig held her tongue. And that's when the first tendrils of fear crept up Jackson's spine. Brig was never quiet. She always spoke her mind.

Unless she didn't want him to know what was on her mind. Unless she was having second thoughts about their marriage. She was finally seeing him as he truly was, a washed-up soldier whose parts were no longer in working order.

"I'm afraid you're not going to be able to walk out of here," the doctor was saying. "You'll be in a wheelchair for weeks, maybe months. After the surgery, you'll be lucky to get around with a cane."

Jackson balled his hands into a fist. He was surprised to find pain coming from his knuckles. But then he looked down at the torn skin where he'd decked the guy who'd come onto Brig. Was this going to be his life? Having to take shots at all the young bucks who sniffed around his young wife? And now he'd have to do that from a wheelchair. Or, if he was lucky, with the assistance of a cane.

"Mr. Bennett? Mr. Bennett, did you hear me?"

Jackson did not hear the doctor. The man's opinion didn't matter. The only person whose opinion mattered was being uncharacteristically silent.

And then, finally, she spoke. "Thank you, Dr. Pierce. We'll take your prognosis under advisement."

The man gave them both a wane smile before turning and leaving the room. The door to the hospital room shut. Jackson and Brig were alone.

Brig took a deep, audible breath. She let it out slow through her parted lips. Jackson tried to hold his breath so that he wouldn't sample any of the sweet air, but his body ignored him. He breathed her in, the scent of cherries, and sugar, and Brig.

"The first thing we're going to do is get a second opinion," she said.

Jackson stared at her lovely face. His immediate thought wasn't how young she looked. It was how vibrant and full of life she appeared. Brigadear Silver oozed vitality and health. She had it in spades.

"We'll start with Dr. Vargas at the university. She's not a surgeon, but I'd trust her prognosis before his. That kid looked barely out of freshman year of college."

Part of Jackson wanted to laugh. Brig thought that kid was young. He was definitely older than her.

"I do think you should spend the night here. I don't want to move you again and make it worse."

"I'll stay," said Jackson. "But you should go."

"I'm not leaving you alone here."

"Visiting hours will be over soon."

"They have to let me stay." Brig shrugged, pulling up a chair to the bed. "I'm going to be your wife."

She took his hand. Her fingers brushed over the torn skin of his knuckles. The skin torn when he'd roughed up the guy who had hit on her earlier tonight.

Jackson shouldn't have let that young buck get under his skin. But he had because the jerk had voiced Jackson's fear. And now that fear had a hold on his knee. It was that fear that had taken Jackson down. And now, he might not be able to stand back up.

"No," Jackson said, his voice strained. "No, you're not."

"I'm not what?" Brig lifted her hand from his knuckles to run them down the side of his face.

It took everything in Jackson to pull away from her touch. "You're not going to be my wife."

Brig jerked back as though he'd slapped her. He felt the sting all over his body. On the positive side, it momentarily muted the pain in his leg.

"You're going to marry Carter as planned. Unless he finally realizes he's in love with Tilly. Then I'll force Truman to do it."

"You'll force someone to marry me?"

"Yes. It's the only way I have left to protect you."

Brig stood. The chair toppled back with the force of the action. "I don't need protection. I need the man I love to come to his senses."

Jackson shut his eyes. It was the second time she'd said she loved him. He hadn't even said it once yet. But it was there in his heart.

Jackson loved Brig. He loved her so much that he knew he couldn't consign her to a life with him if he couldn't be the man she needed.

"You're being serious?" Her voice was quiet. Pain laced every word she said.

The throbbing in his knee was nothing compared to having to cause pain to the woman he would lay down his life for. But he couldn't even get up to do that act for her.

He knew better than to argue with her. Brig was the most intelligent person he knew. She would talk him blue in the face, trying to convince him to her way of thinking. Or worse, she might pull out the heavy artillery and lean down and kiss him. If she did that, all would be lost, and she would be stuck with a man who would never be her match.

"Nurse," Jackson called out to the woman in scrubs passing by the door.

The nurse ducked her head into the room, a pleasant smile on her face. "Do you need something?"

"She needs to go." Jackson chucked a thumb at Brig.

"Isn't this your wife?" asked the nurse.

"No, she's not. She's just a kid."

This time Brig looked like he'd punched her in the gut. Tears stung her eyes. Jackson had hit her where he knew it would hurt the most. But he'd had to do it. She would realize it in time. He was broken, and his path to healing was rocky at best.

Brig would heal. She was young and resilient. She gazed down at him, blue eyes wide and percep-tive as always.

Did she know what he was doing? Did she understand why? Would she ever forgive him?

Jackson wouldn't find out. Brig shuttered her gaze. Then she turned her back on him and marched out the door.

CHAPTER TWENTY

rig knew what Jackson was doing. She'd had enough psychology classes to understand the male mind. Especially when said mind was vulnerable and backed against a wall.

Jackson was protecting himself. Even worse, he thought he was protecting her. In a sense, it was logical. But Jackson's words to her still hurt the next morning.

She lay wrapped up in his sheets in Gunny's cabin. Even though his scent brought her comfort, she couldn't stop hearing the sound of his agony when he'd gone down on the dance floor of the bar.

Brig curled into a fetal position. She brought her legs up to her chest and hugged herself tight.

It brought no comfort. The only thing that

would bring her relief was Jackson's arms wrapped around her. But he was too wrapped up in his own pain to do that.

Well, he'd have to get over that, and quick. In fact, he'd have to do it today. This minute. Because last night and the distance between the ranch and the hospital was all the space she was going to give him.

The only reason she'd left him last night was because she wanted him to feel the pain of pushing her away. Of course, then they'd both been left in agony. Him in a hospital bed with his knee in turmoil. Her in his bed, tossing and turning all night.

It was childish. If they were going to act like children, then they should at least suffer their punishment together.

Brig heard the sound of the door opening. She sat up in the bed, heart pounding that Jackson had come after her. This was the precedent she wanted to set in their relationship, that she was always right.

She breathed a sigh of relief as she sat up. All would be well. They would get married and laugh this off as their first fight.

Then reality dawned. Jackson's knee was too

banged up. He couldn't walk out of the hospital, much less into the cabin.

"She's in here," called Scout.

Brig flopped back down on the bed. Then she pulled the pillow over her head. When she did, she got another strong whiff of Jackson. She felt the urge to punch the pillow. If only that would knock some sense into the man.

"Everything's going to be okay, sweetie," cooed Saylor. The bed dipped as her sister's weight landed on the mattress, and warm hands came to Brig's back.

Brig wanted to tell her sister she didn't need coddling. But the moment Saylor sat down on the bed, Brig found her head migrate to her sister's lap. Her arms went around Saylor's waist, and tears welled up again.

"He sent me away," Brig sniffed. "He said he won't marry me now. He said he's not man enough for me."

"That's the stupidest thing I ever heard," said Scout, fists on her hips as though she were preparing for battle.

"It's kinda romantic," said Mareen.

Scout shot her sister daggers with her eyes.

Mareen held up her hands in placation. Though when Mareen turned from Scout, her eyes rolled.

There was a part of Brig that wanted to laugh at the two. Scout's way of fighting was to shout and bully her opponent into submission. Mareen used the silent treatment and cold shoulder. Neither of their methods ever worked. Scout would eventually tire herself out while Mareen would inevitably get lonely. In the end, they would always wind up talking things out to solve the problem—even if that chat was years in the making.

"I think what Mareen said makes sense," said Tilly.

Now Scout turned her loud glare on Tilly. Mareen turned back around with a warm smile on her face that said *I told you so*. Tilly, used to both their antics, ignored them and focused on Brig.

"Jackson wants what's best for you," Tilly continued. "Now that he's injured, he doesn't believe he's it anymore."

"If he truly believes that," said Scout, "then he's not the man for my baby sister."

"I'm not a kid anymore," said Brig. The pounding of her fist against the mattress didn't help her argument.

"We know that," said Scout. "You haven't been a kid since you said your first word."

"It was cornucopia," grinned Saylor.

It was. Toddler Brig had been fascinated by the horn that overflowed with colorful fruits and corn. She'd grown up in a family full of people, and she was used to being surrounded and wanting for nothing.

"I didn't know that," said Mareen, her voice barely audible.

Mareen had missed a lot. But she was here now. Right in the middle of this overflowing room of sisters. Sisters who would always have her back, even if she tried to turn away. Sisters who would never let her fall anytime she stumbled. Sisters who would stand by as she touched the fire they told her was hot because they'd let her learn her lesson, but they'd never let her get truly hurt.

That's what family did. Whether by blood, or by vow, or by enlistment.

Jackson had enlisted to join this family. He didn't get to suffer on his own. He didn't get to soldier a burden by himself. He was a Silver now, and he'd have to get with the program. Because he needed her. He needed all of them.

Jackson didn't know it, but very soon, his

hospital room would be overflowing with his new family.

"We need to get back to the hospital," said Brig as she threw off the covers.

"I'm driving," said Scout.

"What if he won't see her?" asked Mareen.

"We're not giving him a choice," said Scout. "He wanted in this family, he's in. You don't get out that easily."

"Breaking knees is usually how the mafia let's someone go," said Tilly.

"No, it's putting them in a trunk and parking it in Long Term Parking at the airport," said Scout.

"You've watched way too much *Sopranos*," said Tilly.

"Jackson's in pain right now, Brig," said Saylor. "He's not thinking clearly. Maybe we should give him some time."

"We don't have a lot of time," said Brig. "The will—"

"Don't worry about the will," said Scout. "No matter what, we will always be a family. No matter where we are or who we marry."

"Is everybody decent?" asked a male voice.

When no response came, Carter poked his curly head in the bedroom door. Instead of his gaze going to Tilly, it searched out and found Brig. When his gaze latched onto hers, Brig took a step back.

Jackson said he wanted Brig to marry Carter. Was Carter here to finally make good on that promise? No. Carter's gaze looked worried, not resigned to marrying a woman he didn't love.

"What's wrong?" said Brig. "Is he okay?"

"They're moving him," said Carter.

Relief warmed Brig through, and she took a step forward. "He's coming home?"

"He's not coming back to the ranch," said Carter. "He's checking in at the VA clinic in the city."

CHAPTER TWENTY-ONE

*J*ackson winced as the transport set him down on pavement. His leg was extended and immobilized while in the wheelchair, but he could still feel every bit of loose gravel on the pavement as he was rolled into the VA clinic.

He'd called in the last few favors he had left in the military and had gotten the transfer rushed through. He knew he wouldn't have much reprieve before Brig came back. Jackson knew she would come back, and the next time would be with reinforcements.

Not the President's Men. They knew better than to try to change his mind. Jackson knew Brig would return with a far more formidable weapon; her sisters.

If his brothers wouldn't be enough to change his mind, he knew that the Silver sisters would twist his arm right along with his leg until he cried uncle. He'd expect nothing less of the general's daughters, which was why he'd moved fast. Or as fast as the red-taped, backed up, weighed down healthcare system would allow him to.

Then there was the tangled web of Brigadear Silver. Just another flash of her smile would cut through all the bureaucratic defenses Jackson had armed himself with. Seeing her lip tremble had hurt him, likely more than it had hurt her. But Jackson knew the woman he loved; he knew that pushing her aside might bring her down, but it wouldn't knock her out.

Brig was too strong, too smart to fall for the act for long. She'd be back. Without a vow between them, she wouldn't be able to get in to see him.

The valves of his heart twisted inside his cold chest. The pain was worse than what was going on in his knee. The damage to his knee could be fixed. The pain in his heart would be permanent.

Jackson pounded at his chest to hush the protests within. He knew that wheeling around and racing back to the ranch wasn't best for Brig. She needed a man who could protect her, who could keep pace with her. He could do none of those things.

He also knew that Brig would roll right over Carter if he took her hand. She would race mental circles around Truman if he stepped in. Still, both those men were better options than him.

Inside the waiting area, Jackson saw the fruits of war. Men and women with hands to heads and pain in their features likely suffering from undiagnosed TBIs. Others sat with missing limbs. Many stood alone in corners, no family or friends by their sides. One man caught Jackson's gaze.

He was in a wheelchair. Both his legs were missing and replaced with prosthetics. He held a wiggling child in his muscled arms. Behind him, a vibrant red-haired woman pushed the back of his chair to set the family in motion.

The wounded soldier looked up at her, love in his gaze. The woman, his wife, if the dazzling ring on her finger had anything to say about it, looked down at him the same way. The child gurgled between them, making happy sounds as he looked up at his parents.

A toy tank wheeled into their paths. The man's free hand went to the handbrake on the wheel. The toy tank passed by with another toddler chasing after it. The child's parent gave an apologetic wince as she scooped up both her child and the toy.

The red-haired wife gave the woman a grin and then leaned down and kissed her husband. The child rested a tired head against his father's chest and began to doze. The family continued on out the door as though nothing had happened.

Jackson stared after them.

He'd seen similar scenes at his time on The Purple Heart Ranch. Dylan, who had one leg amputated, and his wife Maggie chasing after dogs and children. Reed, who had had a prosthetic arm, holding his infant in one hand while tapping away at a computer code with the other. Nothing physical stood in the way of those relationships. The men and women who made their lives on the Purple Heart Ranch were some of the strongest Jackson had ever encountered.

Jackson looked down at his knee as he sat in the waiting room. The joint throbbed, though no weight or pressure was on it. He might be in this chair for a long time. He might have to depend on a cane for the rest of his life.

If he remained in the chair, Brig would likely insist on riding on his lap as he wheeled them along.

If he had to rely on the cane, she'd probably decorate the device, and they'd ride horseback most places.

But Brig wasn't here. He'd told her to go. And she had.

He'd put another obstacle in their path. First, with the years between them. And now with his knee.

Jackson came to a horrified realization; he'd blown it. He was the toy tank whizzing between them. An obstruction that might cause him a moment's discomfort, but it would not have taken him down permanently. No, he'd done that all by himself.

"Sir, are you checking in?" A tired-looking man behind the reception counter called to him. He had a clipboard in one hand and a pen in the other.

Jackson wasn't interested in taking either. He wheeled his chair around and headed for the exit. His knee throbbed from the quick action, but he ignored it. He would spend the rest of his life in pain if he didn't correct his mistake.

When he got outside, he realized the mistakes were coming at him from more directions. He didn't have a car. Even if he did, he couldn't drive himself anywhere with the state he was in.

Add to that that he didn't have a cellphone. He

hadn't seen it, much less thought about it, since he'd collapsed onto the dance floor last night. He'd have to go back inside and ask the receptionist to use the phone to call the ranch.

As his hands moved down to the wheels of the chair to turn himself around, Jackson saw two familiar trucks pull up to the front of the clinic. The trucks swerved to a stop, lining up side by side as only stunt car drivers, or a trained unit, could pull off. It was his unit and the Silver sisters.

Brig stumbled as she got out of the truck before the engine was shut off. Jackson wanted to shout at her to be careful, to look both ways before crossing the street, to hurry on over into his arms because he couldn't get to her fast enough.

But Carter caught her. His hand wrapped around her upper arm, and he pulled her back to him. Jackson saw red.

His body demanded he stand. To take his friend down and claim what was his. A second later, Jackson's view of both Brig and Carter was blocked off when an ambulance wailed by them.

Once the danger passed, Brig and Jackson's eyes locked. Jackson held out his arms—but not before looking both ways down the street. Brig's head didn't swivel in either direction. Her gaze was only for him. She ran into his arms, climbing onto his lap just as he had dreamed she would.

"I'm sorry," he said, breathing in her scent of sweetness and sunshine.

"Good," she huffed into his chest. "Because you were an idiot."

Jackson didn't disagree with her. Because, as per usual, Brig was right. Jackson chuckled, and then he groaned in pain.

Brig hopped up off his lap. She looked down at his legs, blue eyes narrowed in that clinical assessment that Jackson found hot. His pain forgotten, he reached for her again. The tears in her eyes cooled his ardor.

"I am an idiot," he said.

Brig's head cocked to the side in the universal language of *duh*.

"But I was also right last night," Jackson continued. "I'm not the man you need."

Brig's eyes closed, pain raining down her features like clouds moving in to storm all over a parade. Jackson reached for her hands. He gave a tug, but she didn't come to him easily. For the first time since he'd known her, Brig resisted his pull.

"I'm not the man you need," he repeated. "But I

want to be. I will be. If you'll be patient with me while I grow up."

Brig still hadn't opened her eyes, but she let out a low sigh. It sounded like relief. It had to be since the pain that had crisscrossed her features a moment ago was quickly evaporating.

And then she was gone.

The wheels of Jackson's chair were set in motion. Brig had disappeared behind him and was now propelling him into the clinic.

What did this mean? Was she trying to get rid of him? Was she finally giving up on him?

"Let's get your knee fixed," Brig said. "I don't want there to be any excuses when I knock you down the next time you try to run from me."

"Won't ever happen again. A man can't run without his beating heart."

The chair jerked as though the person pushing it had stumbled. Brig quickly recovered and pushed harder. The hard push resulted in a jolt of pain in Jackson's knee.

"Ouch," he groaned.

"Serves you right," Brig muttered. "You have to work on your maturity. I have to work on my bedside manner."

"We'll figure it out, baby."

"Okay, boomer."

Brig leaned down and brushed a kiss over Jackson's lips. The pain in his knee didn't magically disappear. It throbbed away, demanding all of his attention. But Jackson was too happy to pay it any mind.

He finally had something to fight for, something that made him feel like a man again. He pulled Brig closer and deepened the kiss. Soon they would cut open and replace parts of his knee. That was fine with him because now he knew the reason he would one day stand tall again was because of the woman who had brought him to his knees in the first place.

EPILOGUE

"I just find most women can't live up to my high expectations."

"Maybe because they're too busy looking down at you?"

Carter snorted into his glass as he eavesdropped on the couple at the table next to him. It was a hilarious thing for the guy to say to the woman who easily had a foot on him. The blonde across from the short stack was a knockout, a woman who was beyond any man's expectations.

As though she'd heard his thoughts, Tilly glanced up at Carter. She narrowed her gaze at him, giving him a sharp glare. In response, Carter grinned back at her.

"I think you're different, Artie," her date was saying.

Tilly's attention snapped back to… whatever his name was. The man had deigned to ignore her nickname and give her one of his liking. That was one of his many mistakes tonight. This date was going to crash in burn in a matter of minutes. Like he had been doing for the past two months, Carter would be there to pick up the pieces.

"You're pretty enough. You were early for our date, which shows eagerness. You ordered a steak, which shows me you're healthy. But you'll need to cut back on the calories before things get out of hand and you balloon up. I won't be one of those husbands who'll stand to let his wife go after I put a ring on it."

Carter snorted again. He grabbed his dinner napkin and dabbed at his face. But a few other diners looked over at him. One woman half rose from her seat as though she were eager to give him mouth to mouth CPR. Carter sat his dinner napkin down and smiled politely at the eager woman.

The woman took a step towards him. But a white flag went flying through the air. The dinner napkin landed on the floor.

Carter stared at it for a moment. It was Tilly's

signal. She'd had enough of her date and it was time for him to step in and save her. Or save her date from being strangled. Whichever.

Giving the woman who wanted to resuscitate him an apologetic grimace, Carter bent his form to pick up Tilly's napkin. "Excuse me, ma'am, I think you dropped... Artillery? Artillery Silver, is that you?"

"I'm sorry," Tilly pressed her hand to her chest. "Do we know each other?"

"Do we know each other?" Carter turned and gave her date a chuckle. "How could you forget me? We met at fat camp when we were teens. Don't you remember?"

There was a sputtering cough. It didn't come from Tilly or Carter. Tilly's date was choking on his drink after Carter's pronouncement of Tilly as a formerly overweight person. Carter didn't hear the flimsy excuse the man gave to get out of there.

Carter used the discarded white dinner napkin to dust off the vacated chair. He was mildly surprised that he didn't see a puddle in the seat after the occupant's hasty retreat.

"Can you believe the nerve of that guy? Not one thing from his profile was true." Tilly poured herself another glass of wine from the opened bottle on the table. She tilted the bottle to Carter, but he put his hand over the top of the glass nearest him. "Right, I keep forgetting your one glass rule."

Carter hadn't finished the glass that was still sitting on the other table. He'd never been much of a drinker. In any of its forms, alcohol tasted the same to him; like a bitter astringent that was best used to strip a car's engine. As he watched Tilly's throat work to take the liquid down, he began to feel a thirst that he knew the red liquid would never quench.

When Tilly dabbed at her lip to catch a wayward droplet of the red ambrosia, Carter looked away. It wasn't the alcohol he wanted. No, he wanted something he had never tasted, could never taste.

A tremor ran down the length of his right arm, causing his index finger to tremble. He clenched his fingers around the fork to hide it from her. Tilly was usually a very observant woman, but he'd managed to keep the occasional shakes and twitches from her over the past two months.

"You're being too hard on..." Carter paused. "What was his name again?"

Tilly opened her mouth to respond. Then she frowned. "I gave up trying to remember after he told me my figure reminded him of his mother."

Carter's gaze went from the red stains on her bottom lip, to the crinkle between her brow. The little lines that drew in there formed the center point of a heart where the two halves met in the middle. Her blue eyes rounded at the top part of the heart. Her bottom lip completed the shape.

Oh no. He was back looking at her mouth again. He had to stop doing that; looking at Artillery Silver's perfectly kissable lips was mission impossible. Because he was never going to kiss those lips. He'd never know how soft they were, or if they were sweeter than the wine she sipped.

"That's sad," he said. "You don't know the name of your future husband."

Tilly scowled at and snatched the fork away from him.

That single touch sent a jolt of awareness through him. Carter's pinky finger joined the fluttering dance of his index finger. To hide the involuntary movement, he returned to his table to grab his own cutlery. By the time he took his seat across from Tilly again, his fingers were behaving.

When he looked up, he found Tilly's gaze on him. She wasn't looking at his hands. She was looking at his face.

That furrowed frown turned into a pointed

glare. What Tilly didn't know was that Carter found that her glare made her even more beautiful. Her blue eyes blazed like the hottest part of the fire, making Carter want to forget any caution and get burned.

"He probably lied about his name, too," Tilly huffed. "How can you trust someone who misleads you or keeps secrets?"

A spasm rocketed through Carter's palm. He dropped the fork, letting it clatter to the plate. Then he shoved his trembling hand under the table like the dirty little secret it was.

Tilly had been carving a piece of meat. Her gaze tracked to the edge of the table where his hand had disappeared. She pursed her lips as though she were about to ask him what the matter was?

"Was it the height or the bald head that did it?" Carter needled, trying to get her attention back on her awful date.

"I have nothing against a bald head. Look at Vin Diesel, or the Rock. And what modern woman hasn't had a fantasy or two about Peter Dinklage in his role as Tyrion Lannister?"

"Peter Dinklage? I thought you would've been a Warwick Davis kinda girl."

"Why would you think that?"

"You made me watch Willow last weekend."

"Made you?" she scoffed. "You're the one that swore that Val Kilmer hit his peak as Doc Holliday in Tombstone. I had to counter that with the brilliance of his acting in the role of Madmartigan."

"Proving once again that you like the villain to turn into a hero."

The frown was back. It always came back when he'd bested Tilly in the language she knew best; filmology.

"Let's face it, you're the only woman I know whose favorite John Cusack film isn't Say Anything."

"Because it's a sappy 80s film."

"You and your dark heart love Grosse Pointe Blank."

She grinned at the mention of her favorite film. "Who in their right mind doesn't love that film? Rebel son returns to his hometown for his high school reunion where everyone else has a family, a house, and a dog. But Martin Blank has become a professional hitman with a score to settle because he was an overachiever."

Carter chuckled. Trust Tilly to find the good in a trained assassin. She would've been perfect for his best friend Truman, who was an actual trained sniper. But the thought of Truman holding Tilly set his entire arm to shaking.

"I'm surprised you didn't go that route," Tilly said.

"What? An assassin? Unlike our hero in your favorite film, when I took the Army's psych exam, it showed that my moral compass was pointed due North."

"How lucky for Gunny."

The mention of Tilly's twin was like a bomb between them. A tremor went through Carter's entire body and a piercing pain in his head made him wince.

"You're still on board to marry her, right?" asked Tilly. "I mean, now that Brig and Jackson are together, she's the only one of us left."

"And you." Carter pressed his lips together. He hadn't meant to say that out loud. But the two words hung between them.

"I'll be fine." Tilly waved away the inconvenience of her single state in the face of only three weeks before the deadline to keep their family ranch. "I've got a few more dates lined up. I'm sure one of them has to be my Mr. Right."

"Yeah, sure." Carter's tone lacked any kind of

certainty. "Or you could run after your date. I'm sure he hasn't gotten that far."

Tilly tossed her dinner napkin at him. Carter caught the white flag. He wished it meant her surrender.

But it didn't. Tilly saw him as a friend. In truth, that's all he could ever be to her. She was already close enough to him that she might see the secrets he was hiding from her, from everyone. At least when he married Gunny, that particular Silver sister would only stick around long enough for the ink of the wedding license to dry. Then she'd be off, returning to her quest to save the world, and all its endangered species.

The upside to the deal was that Carter would have a place to stay, a place to work, and he'd still get to hang out with Tilly and watch movies, or talk about nonsense. He couldn't ask for much more than that in this life. It was likely more than he deserved.

This date is going to end with a kiss;
a kiss between Carter and Tilly!

*But you won't believe what happens after these two share
their first kiss.
It's the stuff of movie magic complete with a music
montage from a boom box blaring a Peter Gabriel ballad!
You don't want to miss "His Pledge to Have,"
Book Five from the Silver Star Ranch romances.*

Shanae Johnson was raised by Saturday Morning cartoons and After School Specials. She still doesn't understand why there isn't a life lesson that ties the issues of the day together just before bedtime. While she's still waiting for the meaning of it all, she writes stories to try and figure it all out. Her books are wholesome and sweet, but her are heroes are hot and heroines are full of sass!

And by the way, the E elongates the A. So it's pronounced Shan-aaaaaaaa. Perfect for a hero to call out across the moors, or up to a balcony, or to blare outside her window on a boombox. If you hear him calling her name, please send him her way!

You can sign up for Shanae's Reader Group and receive a FREE NOVELLA in this world at

http://bit.ly/ShanaeJohnsonReaders

Also By Shanae Johnson

The Silver Star Ranch Romances

His Pledge to Honor

His Pledge to Cherish

His Pledge to Protect

His Pledge to Obey

His Pledge to Have

His Pledge to Hold

The Rangers of Purple Heart

The Rancher takes his Convenient Bride

The Rancher takes his Best Friend's Sister

The Rancher takes his Runaway Bride

The Rancher takes his Star Crossed Love

The Rancher takes his Love at First Sight

The Rancher takes his Last Chance at Love

The Brides of Purple Heart

On His Bended Knee

Hand Over His Heart

Offering His Arm

His Permanent Scar

Having His Back

In Over His Head

Always On His Mind

Every Step He Takes

In His Good Hands

Light Up His Life

Strength to Stand

The Rebel Royals series

The King and the Kindergarten Teacher

The Prince and the Pie Maker

The Duke and the DJ

The Marquis and the Magician's Assistant

The Princess and the Principal